MW01491705

LITTLE NECK

DARCIE DENNIGAN

Fonograf Editions
Portland, OR

Copyright © 2025 • Darcie Dennigan • All rights reserved
Cover and text design by Mike Corrao

Cover art: *Anémone de Mer* by Jean Painlevé, courtesy of
    Archives Jean Painlevé in Paris, France

First Edition, First Printing

FONO39

Published by Fonograf Editions
www.fonografeditions.com

For information about permission to reuse any material from this
book, please contact Fonograf Ed. at info@fonografeditions.com.

Distributed by NYU Press
NYUPress.org

[clmp]

Fonograf Editions is a proud member of the Community
of Literary Magazines and Presses

ISBN: 978-1-964499-51-2
ISBN (ebook): 978-1-964499-53-6
LCCN: 2024926476

With thanks to Cill Rialaig for the Ballinskelligs residency, and
to William Walsh, Farnoosh Fathi, Aleksandar Bošković, and
Julia Jarcho. Thanks to Kate Schapira ten times over. This book
is dedicated to Kate Colby.

LITTLE NECK

FONOGRAF EDITIONS

THOUGH THOU BE SOUGHT FOR

YET SHALT THOU NEVER BE

FOUND AGAIN

$\mathcal{N}$OW THAT I AM MARGUERITE CONCRETE, I KNOW IT IS Rosmarge who chose the epitaph. *Now go*. It is a thing that Rosmarge would say and it is the way she would say it. *Now go*. The gravestone has a first name. Pearl. No last name. No dates. It has only a first name and an epitaph. Pearl. *Now go*.

You're early. That is what Rita says to me. It is my first day at Marguerite Concrete. And then Rita says to me, Are you going to miss your groundskeeper. I say nothing. And Rosmarge says nothing. Only coughs. Rosmarge and Rita are the two sisters of Marguerite Concrete. They are both stonecutters and Rosmarge is a carver too. They wet the stone before they cut it but the dust still kills their voices. Their voices sound sandy. When they cough it sounds like stones are loose in their throats. Are you going to miss your groundskeeper. Rita says that and

Rosmarge coughs. When Rita says that her eyes are big and very bright. When she is done saying that her eyes go back to being small. And dusty. Are you going to miss your groundskeeper. Then Rita says to Rosmarge, Remember them talking about her. Rita is looking at me and talking to Rosmarge. Half of Little Neck talking about her. And Rosmarge laughs. Her laugh is like a cough. This is my first day at Marguerite Concrete. The sisters have put me on a long couch in the side room. It is August. It is only August. I am not supposed to come to Marguerite Concrete until winter. But I wake up in the side room and the sisters are there and Rita says, You're early. And she asks me about the keeper. Am I going to miss him. What is it that I call him. Not, What do you call him. But, What is it that you call him. I do not answer. This is the only day that the sisters ask me questions about him. This is the only day they say *keeper*. Or *groundskeeper*. They do not say those words again. After that first day they never say a word about him. My wrist is still bleeding. Rita asks questions. Rosmarge seems to already know the answers. I do not talk. My wrist is bleeding a lot. I am not going to talk about the keeper. I am not going to talk. I am never going to say a thing at all. The sisters are very interested in the cut on my wrist. I think at first it is because they are cutters. All day they cut stone. And Rosmarge carves. They are interested in any sharp thing that cuts well. And the glass that cuts my wrist cuts it well. The cut does not stop bleeding. For days it is bleeding. They put ice on my wrist to slow the blood. That is a stonecutters' trick. But the blood keeps coming. When their ice does not work I am glad. I want the cut to bleed. Until the blood runs under the door of Marguerite Concrete and down the road. Half a mile seaward. To Rose Head. A line of my blood half a mile long. The keeper sees the blood running down the road through the cemetery's east cape. He kneels and touches a finger to it. He puts that finger in his mouth.

On the second day the bleeding stops. But then it starts again. Rosmarge holds more ice to the cut and says to Rita, That Pearl. Still a troublemaker. And Rita laughs. And Rosmarge coughs. Their voices are both terrible. Then I know two things. The sisters know who Pearl is. A troublemaker is what they say. So they know who Pearl is when she is alive. And they know about my last night at Rose Head. That it is at Pearl's grave where my wrist gets cut. Rosmarge holds my wrist tightly. She smells like a stone. And Rita like a warmer stone. Rosmarge's voice is sharper than Rita's. She is the carver and the elder sister. Both sisters cut the slate and Rosmarge carves the words and ornaments. It is the second day. Rita is saying to Rosmarge, She is just there. She is just there in the dirt. Rita isn't laughing. She says it again, She is just there in the dirt. Each time Rita says this, Rosmarge's fingers on my wrist get stronger. Four fingertips on my skin and her thumb on the cut. Her knuckles have yellow crusts. Rita says it again, She is just there in the dirt. Rosmarge pushes her thumb into the cut. She pushes her thumb all the way in and touches my wrist bone. Then Rita says it one more time and Rosmarge's thumb presses into my wrist bone and the bone bruises. Is it me Rita means. Does she mean that she knows about me being at Pearl's grave and digging it up and fainting there. That the keeper tells her where and how he finds me. The sisters talk like they know Pearl. They know Pearl. And they know about me digging all the way into her grave and touching one of her bones. Or is Rita speaking of Pearl. Does she know there is no box. Does she know the body at Pearl's stone is not in a box. It is loose. In pieces. In the dirt. My last night at Rose Head I am digging at Pearl's grave and I touch one of her bones. Her wrist bone. Rita's voice is worse than Rosmarge's. It is higher. She is saying, In the dirt, In the dirt. Rosmarge is saying nothing. Her saying nothing is better than saying stop. Rita stops. Then Rosmarge says to Rita, And this one too. This one in the dirt too. Right there in the grave in the same dirt. Now Rosmarge is talking about me. So the sisters know Pearl is not buried in a box. And either they see me that night at Rose Head in Pearl's grave or the keeper tells them how he finds me. And then Rosmarge says more. She does not say much so what she does say is important. She says something to Rita. She says, But he didn't get her.

On the third day Rita makes the bleeding stop. For good. I go to sleep. I lie on the long couch all winter. I lie on my back like the dead do. *He didn't get her.* My first winter at Marguerite Concrete I think *he* is the keeper. Do they mean the keeper did not get me. That the keeper does not get to touch me. Or he does not get to keep me. I want him to come to the door of the stonehouse and take me back to the cemetery. I want him to get me and he does not. There are long-stemmed mushrooms that come up at the edges of Rose Head after the rain. I fit five of the mushroom stems in my mouth. The keeper comes up the hill. He stops. He does not say the words, What are you doing. His eyes ask the question. He does not say any words. I take the stems out of my mouth and I do not look at him and I do not say, Your fingers. *One from the other.* Your fingers. *Watch between me and thee while we are absent one from the other.* The sisters do not say who *he* is. *He* is not something they talk about. It is not something they do not talk about. It is dust covering everything they say. The dust in the stonehouse of Marguerite Concrete sucks the wet out of the air. My mouth is dry and my eyes and throat. Rosmarge's and Rita's faces have a large space for their eyes but their eyeballs are small. The dust dries and shrinks the balls of their eyes. Rita is the talker at Marguerite Concrete. When she opens the door the fresh air gets in her eyes. The wet fresh air mixes with the dust in her eyes and she cries stones. I lie on the bed in the side room. I can see Rita at the counter but I can't see who is at the door or who is on the other side of the counter. Only Rita. The bereaved must like it when Rita opens the door and right away her eyes cry stones. They must see her as a real stonecutter. Even her tears are stone. All winter Rosmarge checks on my wrist. She touches the cut and says to Rita, Here's a real carver. I don't know who the real carver is. Does she think I mean to cut my wrist. Or that Pearl in her grave cuts it. She says, Here's a real carver. Then she coughs. That is how she laughs. The dust from Marguerite Concrete kills the sisters' throats. Rosmarge does not have a laugh anymore only a cough. And when the sisters talk it sounds like their voices are coming up through concrete. On my second day here when my wrist starts bleeding again the sisters try ice. It does not work and it does not work. Then Rita says, There's always the cement. Rosmarge looks at her. When she looks at someone it is not for her to see their face but for them to see hers. The cement is in the backroom of Marguerite Concrete. Rita says there used to be bags and bags. When the sisters are younger they make cement in a secret way. Everyone wants the cement they make. They make it in a secret way and it is the best cement in Little Neck. And farther. The sisters mix it with pebbles and water to make the famous Marguerite Concrete. And with this famous concrete they make gravestones. Before the sisters and their cement the cemetery has slate graves. Most graves at Rose Head are slate. When the sisters start with their concrete then everyone in Little Neck gets a concrete grave. All up the coast too, Rita says. But then one of the ingredients in their cement goes away and they can't make the famous concrete anymore. They go back to making slate graves. And that, says Rita, is that. And now there are only two bags of cement left. The sisters are keeping a bag each for when they die. They are going to be dead with their names in concrete. For now they are cutting and carving slate again. There is plenty of slate from the quarry. Little Neck is a quarry town. But I am not going to have a slate grave. Or any stone. I have already had my gravestone. It is when I am born. When I am born I am left by a gravestone at Rose Head. Rita says to me that half of Little Neck wonders which grave. When she says this I can tell that she and Rosmarge know which one. The sisters only want to know if I know it too. On the second day at Marguerite Concrete when my wrist starts bleeding again the sisters try ice. Then Rita says, There's always the cement. And Rosmarge looks at her. She doesn't want to use their famous cement. Rita leaves the sideroom and comes back with a handful of it. Rosmarge looks at her in a sharp way and Rita says, It's mine, I took it from my bag. Then she sprinkles the cement across my cut. Cement sucks up anything wet. The cement dust mixes with my blood. Concrete forms. It burns and melts the skin around the cut. And then there is a scab. It is skin and concrete. It is a thick scab but it opens and bleeds when I move my hand. The sisters have to let me rest. I lie on the long couch in the side room. I am there all winter. I ask Rita what the ingredient is in the cement that they can't find anymore. She says it is a secret. And she says they are done looking for it. She says, We are done with the crusher and the kiln. And again, We are done with the crusher and the kiln. And then Rosmarge says, She hath done what she could. It is an epitaph on a few of the graves at Rose Head. Again Rita says, We are done with the crusher and the kiln. Then again Rosmarge says, She hath done what she could. And they both laugh terrible laughs. I am lying down all winter. It looks like I am sleeping. The summer is dead and it is being buried in the winter. The bees in the frozen ground. The green in the brown and gray. Rose Head is being buried by Marguerite Concrete. And then the winter is over. *There will no longer be any mourning or crying or pain. The first things have passed away.* Winter is over and still it is very cold inside. The stonehouse lets no sun in and no cold drafts out. The light inside smells like wet stone. And dust. Rita and Rosmarge are in the front room talking about me. They are saying, She needs to stand up. Her wrist is fine now. She should get up and learn the trade. Now I am standing in front of them. Rosmarge nods at my scar. It looks like a tuber. Though *tuber* is not a word the sisters would say. Or *root.* The scar sticks up from my wrist. A vein of skin but bigger than a vein. A finger of skin. When I am digging at the grave on my last night at Rose Head I do not know that the cut is so deep. It is too dark inside the grave to see. Then I wake up and I am in the stonehouse. And then it is winter and then winter is over and I am standing and Rosmarge is showing me the tools. The hose and the saw. The air hammer. The chisel. Rosmarge says it is not hard to learn. She says it is in my blood. At first I think she means the cement on my wrist has mixed with my blood and now I am part stone. But Rosmarge is trying to tell me I am related to her. I have the same blood as her. She is trying to say it without saying it. That is how the sisters talk. I have been here since the bindweed night. All fall and all winter. I do not go outside. *All flesh is grass.* The sisters smell like dust.

A VOICE SAYS CRY. *WHAT SHALL I CRY.* SOMEONE knocks on the door of Marguerite Concrete. Rosmarge yells, Rita, a bereaved. Rita is the sister who opens the door and talks. She is the nicer sister. And Rosmarge is the smarter one. Rita works in the cutting room until someone knocks. She never hears the knock. Rosmarge can hear but she cannot see well. The dust has cut into Rosmarge's eyes. But she hears. And she yells for Rita. And Rita hurries to the door. But sometimes she forgets the Chantilly and then Rosmarge yells, Rita the Chantilly. *The Chantilly* is what the sisters call it. The piece of black lace that Rita wears around her shoulders when she speaks to the bereaved. It covers her work shirt. It makes her small dry eyes look smaller and darker. Two holes in sick ground. Then the bereaved leaves. Rita hangs the Chantilly on its hook and takes a note with the gravestone's words back to the carver. Who is Rosmarge. And who is now me. It is the day of my first epitaph and the bereaved does not know what to say. *A voice says cry.* Rita is bringing a note to the cutting room with the name of the dead and the dates but no epitaph. Not everyone wants one. But this bereaved wants one. And does not know what to say. *What shall I cry.* When that happens the carver chooses and today I am the carver. It is my wrist that is going to trace and carve the letters. Then rinse the stone. Then strap the stone to the tripod hoist. And then the sisters roll the hoist into the truck to Rose Head. Where the keeper is going to read what I have written. And get me. And come get me.

S. Not an easy letter to make. The *S* is the vine. The bindweed vine curling around Pearl's grave. Its pretty white flowers with their pink stripes. The bindweed's thin leaves with their points turning to the gate. To the road out of Rose Head. I see the bindweed vine in a dream. It is a dream I have on my last night at Rose Head. Though I do not know it is my last night. *Behold the shape my dreams take thereafter.* In the dream I am lying on my stomach in the grass. Pearl's stone at my head. The keeper is walking up the hill towards me. His boots are dragging the grass. I stay still as the dead. If the keeper thinks I am dead he will come close to me. But he does not even see me. He keeps walking. He walks on me thinking I am the grass. The toe of his boot comes down between my legs. Then the heel of the second boot snaps my neck. The neck bones breaking send my eyes up. And I see it. Bindweed. Bindweed crawling across the grave. It loves the salt air. It is the prettiest vine. But it strangles all else. I wake up and leave the chapelhouse and run to the east cape. To the gravestone that says *Pearl*. It is still dark out but I can see the vine. *Behold the shape my dreams take thereafter.* I begin to dig. If a shovels breaks the shoots the weed grows more. Strangles more. So I dig with my hands. I am going to get rid of the bindweed and the keeper is going to see. But then. But then I cut my wrist and wake up at Marguerite Concrete.

U. The crook of a white pine. There are white pines all along the road that leads in from Rose Head's main gate. One of the Touissants wants to be buried beneath a white pine. He wants no embalmer and no box. He wants his body to turn into a part of the tree. But it does not. The Touissants are mostly on the east cape. They have columbines planted near their stones. The Touissants have purple columbine and their dead in boxes and they do not visit each other. The white pines have a cool smell. It is a smell that cools your blood. I drink their sap. It is not sweet. But it is something. It is something to do. The summer of the trouble I do not climb the white pines. I do not want shade. My blood does not want to be cooled. I collect the needles and sleep with them on my pillow. When crushed their smell is sharp. And it is a smell the keeper loves. It makes him open his eyes. More than halfway. His lids are usually half closed. I have not held his eyelids in my hands. But they look heavy. It looks like his lids are holding up a pile of dirt. The summer of the trouble the keeper's lids stay halfway down. Or more. I put the needles on my pillow. Then rest my head on them and sleep. My skull is heavy and it crushes the needles. Their sap leaks into my hair.

The next day he is near me. He smells the coolness and opens his eyes all the way and looks right at me. I stay very still. The way you are still with a bee. When a bee is at your neck. That is the kind of still that the keeper needs. I smell like white pine and I am very still and the keeper opens his eyes all the way and steps very close to me.

M. The sticks after they fall from the oak by the old rock wall. *M* again. At Rose Head I call the sticks the tree's bones.

What is *E.* It is the keeper's hand. His hand reaching out to the right. One day he digs up a gravesite. To bury a mother with her dead child. First the child dies. It is buried. The mother has a stone made. Summers and winters are passing. The child has long passed away. Then the mother dies. She has no people left to buy her a box. No money for a stone. She is going in the paupers' part. The body arrives. I start to walk toward the paupers' part with the tools. The keeper steps in front of me. He reaches his hand out to the right. His hand is reaching toward the hill on the east cape. His hand is the *E.* Reaching toward the child's grave. Where the keeper plants snow glories. They are tiny and pop up in funny places. They always look like they want to play. Even when they're dying. The keeper digs up the child's grave. But the mother's body is too new. It doesn't fit yet in the child's box. He has to dig more. He puts the mother's box at the bottom of the hole and then the child's bones in with the mother's body. *For he will bring every work into judgment, with every secret thing.* Then the keeper burns the child's box.

R. When I carve *R* I think of my scar. What makes a cut like that. That is a question the sisters like to ask each other. They take their coffee in the sideroom where I sleep. And they give each other answers. Rita says, A saw. Rosmarge says, Grass clippers. Then Rita says, Glass. A shard of glass. Rosmarge turns to look at Rita and Rita is quiet. Glass is right. And the sisters know it is. But Rita is not supposed to say the right thing. The sisters think I know something about Pearl. But what I know is not very much. Her body is not buried in a box. Her bones are not close together. And there is glass in the dirt at her grave. After it cuts me I dig it out. Its shape makes me think of lilac. Of half a lilac. A lilac is not a flower I hold by the stem. I make a bowl with my hands and the lilac fills the bowl. A lilac is not like another flower that dies the moment it is picked. It stays alive in the bowl of your hands. Its lilac blood runs up and down its stem. I want to put my face in the bowl and drink it. The glass in Pearl's grave is like half a lilac. Curved and thick. A ball of lilac split along its stem with an ax. I feel a scrape against my wrist. The shard scrapes once when my wrist goes down into the dirt. And again when I pull my wrist out. I dig around for the sharp thing and pull it up and it is not rock but glass. The scar is the R and today I am the carver making words for the keeper to read. *S U M M E R. Summer is coming.*

The quarryman's daughter is here to talk to Rita. She comes on some afternoons and they sit in the front room. I am in the cutting room and I hear the quarryman's daughter ask Rita how I am doing. She says, And the young one… And

Rita says to her quickly, Good good, very good. I want to see the quarryman's daughter. The sisters say she has only one hand. I start to walk into the front room. The face shield is still on me. The gloves and the apron and all the cutting room things are on me. Then Rosmarge has her mouth next to my ear. Oh no you don't. The sisters do not want anyone in Little Neck to see my face. They say, Wouldn't they just love that. And, Half of Little Neck would love to get a look at you. They say the town wants to see who I look like. Not what but who. The sisters are glad that they can see me and the town cannot. At Rose Head I don't see people. The keeper says funerals are for the bereaved. And when the bereaved visit the graves the keeper says, Give them a little space. And now here in Marguerite Concrete I cannot see people. If Little Neck sees me they will know who made me. The sisters think they know who made me. What blood is inside me. They do and they don't say. Oh no you don't, Rosmarge says. I have to go back to the cutting room. But for one second I see the quarryman's daughter and she sees me. She cannot see my face. The shield is on. But she waves as if she knows me. She waves to me with the arm that has no hand.

It is June in the stonehouse. There is a different air through the door crack of Marguerite Concrete. It is muggy out. At Rose Head the skin on the keeper's neck is red and sweating. The midges are back and they are biting the keeper's skin. The gravestone with my writing is done. Is done and delivered. Rosmarge drives the truck down to Rose Head. The keeper has the stone in the tripod hoist. He installs it.

He sees that this carver is different. My letters do not look the same as Rosmarge's. He reads the epitaph. His hands are touching the stone with my writing. *Summer is coming.* The keeper knows what this means. Only the keeper and I know. The sisters think it is not a good epitaph. But the carver chooses and I chose. And the keeper reads it. The midges are around his head. They are biting. The keeper lets them. Sometimes he turns his head. Or lifts his shoulders. The holes on his neck that pour out sweat are the size of a midge. Smaller. The size of the tongue of a midge. I am very close to the keeper. I am a midge putting my whole tongue into the hole where his sweat comes out. I am licking the keeper's sweat but there is too much of it. Licking does not go fast enough. I have to drink his sweat. I am drinking and drinking it. There is not room in my body for all the sweat I am drinking. I die on his neck with my tongue stuck in a hole on his skin. Or I am a swarm. I am a swarm of midges. The keeper is walking through the high grass to the paupers' part. It is dusk. He steps near a puddle. A swarm of me flies up. He is surprised. His lips are open just a little. All of me flies into his mouth. And bites his tongue. Bites until he gags. He has to swallow me. He can't get me down. He tries and coughs. I die in his mouth. He spits me out on the dirt. I die at Rose Head with the keeper's blood in my stomach and his sweat in my mouth. I am listening for his knock. The keeper knocking at the door of Marguerite Concrete. Today the keeper is the bereaved. Bereaved of me. He knocks and it is me who opens the door. The Chantilly around me. The keeper not saying a word. It is better to never say a thing. I open the door and the outside air hits my eyes and the stones roll out. He looks at my eyes crying small stones and turns his chin over his shoulder. It is in the direction of Rose Head. Chin turned but eyes on me. My fingertips are always dry and dusty inside the stonehouse. The keeper looks at me in the doorway and my fingertips darken. My fingertips are dark and wet. There is dirt all over them. I unwrap the Chantilly. I have no workclothes on. There is my collarbone. There are the bones of my shoulders. And there are the peonies. Two peonies where my breasts would be. It is the second time the keeper is seeing them. He keeps his head turned and eyes on me. But then the outside air touches the peonies and they are not real flowers anymore. They are made of dust. The fresh air blows them away. Blows the dust up my nose. There is no message back and there is no message back.

THERE IS A LARGE PUDDLE ON THE CUTTING ROOM FLOOR. Of my making. I am going to see what I look like. And who. I leave the hose on for a long time. There is a good puddle slanting toward the back door. It is time to look at my face. I take off the gloves and then the face mask. I look down at the puddle. The floor of the cutting room is very light. It is light colored cement. I can see myself but not well. I can see that I have a face. It is a face with skin the color of the cutting room floor. This is the face that the town thinks is someone else's face. Then I see Rosmarge. She is standing behind me. I see her mouth in the puddle and it is laughing. I never leave Rose Head and now I never leave Marguerite Concrete. The doors are locked and only the sisters leave and come back. They do not say why. They do not say if it is to keep me in or others out. *He didn't get her.* Rosmarge does not say *Pearl* very much. Which means she wants to. But Rita says that name. And Rita talks about Pearl as if she is still making things happen. And Rosmarge coughs. Or says back, Don't I know. They say enough for me to know that Pearl is the third Marguerite Concrete sister. And that it is Rosmarge who chooses the epitaph for Pearl's grave. For her sister. Pearl. *Now go*. She chooses it because she is the carver. She also chooses it because she is the bereaved. Rita is also the bereaved. And Rita is coming to her own door. Crying stones. Putting the Chantilly around her shoulders to open the door for herself. Or Rosmarge goes out back and comes around to the front door and knocks. And Rita doesn't answer right away. Rosmarge has to yell, Rita, a bereaved. But she yells it from outside the door. And Rita opens the door and the fresh air hits her eyes. She cries stones. Rosmarge is also crying stones. They are the bereaved. Their sister is dead. They make her a stone. They do not say that Pearl is their sister. They do not say things in that way. At first I think *Now go* means that Rosmarge does not like Pearl. *Now go* is a good epitaph. It is a good one. Short and tight. The mouth opens only a little. Then it's over. *Now go*. It is five letters. An easy one to carve. It can be carved in a week. *Now go*. And it can be mean. Scram. *Scram* is what the keeper says to the squirrels when they are eating the bulbs. Scram. And that day with the peonies what he says to me is *Run*. But maybe Rosmarge wants Pearl to stay. Now go. She is smart and tricky and does not say what she means. Now go can mean Come back. Rosmarge says things in that opposite way. Run can mean Stay. Now go can mean Come back. Whose face do I have. At Rose Head there are the greenhouse windows. And the chapelhouse windows.

In the summer of the trouble I look in the windows all of the time. But I am only looking to see how still I can stay. How much like a branch or stem. A stem of blue phlox. And the keeper coming with his fingers to touch me. Rosmarge is behind me. I see her face in the puddle. Her mouth is laughing. Rosmarge has a mean way. But she does things in an opposite way. Her mouth is laughing. The opposite is that her mouth is dying.

The bereaved choose the epitaph. Or the carver can choose if the bereaved have none. And the keeper chooses the flowers. For Pearl's grave the keeper chooses purple coneflowers. Which are strong. They are hard to hurt. But the bindweed at Pearl's stone is killing her coneflowers. Strangling them at their top and down at their roots. The bindweed's pretty white flowers are killing the strong purple ones. Bindweed is very pretty. Thin white petals and a sweet smell. It is so pretty and sweet. And it strangles. When it flowers that means its taproots are already very deep in the dirt. And then there is the night I dig the bindweed up. I dig down into the dirt. I pull up the roots and tubers. I find the end of the bindweed and it is a surprise. The tubers at the end have knuckles. They have knuckles and fingernails. And there are little hairs on the knuckles and dirt under the nails. At the end I pull five tubers. Five fingers that smell like skin. And the tuber fingers are warm. I take the fingers in my hand. Each tuber is a finger on the keeper's hand. In the dark it really can be his hand. I want to put this whole tuber hand in my mouth. It does not fit. I put it on my knee. It is good to feel a hand on my knee. Then I put the hand inside of me. My head is down. The keeper's hand is in me. His whole hand is feeling the temperature in me. The birds are beginning the day. The dirt in Pearl's grave is not cold. His hand is digging up into me. *All lost in thee.* But the glass with the lilac shape has cut me. And the cut on my wrist is deeper than I can see. It does not hurt but I am bleeding a lot. I faint with his hand digging up into me.

It is night. I take the diamond saw. I am very quick. I don't try for the door. It is too far. I try a high window in the cutting room. I plug in the saw and stand on the workbench. I am going to be very quick. Sawing through the window frame. It is loud but Rita does not hear well. And Rosmarge does not move quickly. Sawing through the frame. Going back to Rose Head. Marguerite Concrete is a punishment. A stonehouse with two sisters and slate dust. A year of punishment. It is enough. After the Peggy stone and the peonies the keeper says that this is my last summer at Rose Head. That the day is coming when I have to leave. In the winter he is sending me to Marguerite Concrete. He does not say it is because of the peonies. But I know it is my punishment. *Set me as a seal upon thine arm.* And I do not make it to the winter. I wake up here in August. Marguerite Concrete is my punishment and I grow it myself. I grow it the summer of the trouble. Its seed is a rock. This rock is cold and rough. I make myself stand in the high grass in the paupers' part. Then I push the rock far up in me. When it is all the way in then I lie down. I lie on my stomach. Very still. There is pain. It isn't like the pain of the peonies growing. This pain doesn't want more pain. The rock is not a good pain and so it is a good punishment and I make it myself. But then the rock stays in me too long. It gets warm and hurts less. And then I think of the keeper. His fingers. And then it is not a good punishment. Or it is a good punishment in time. Because this rock is the seed that grows into Marguerite Concrete. I bury the rock in me and it grows. It grows into the stonehouse. In the high grass the rock is inside of me and I am all around it. But the rock grows. Now I am in the middle of it. I am in the Marguerite Concrete stonehouse. The rock is all around me and I have to use the diamond saw to cut myself out. It has been a year almost. I am taller. The keeper is going to look at me. One jamb is cut. I am starting on the sill. I am quick. But the wood is thick. The saw goes off. The plug is not in the wall. The plug is in Rita's hand. She is looking up at me on the bench and talking. She looks small and she is talking a lot. And Rosmarge is laughing. I can't see her but I can hear her cough. Now all the tools are locked at night. The door of the cutting room is locked. *He didn't get her.* I cannot tell what the sisters mean. Who the he is and who the her is. The sisters look old. Their eyes are small and their voices are rough. Their hands are ugly. And their shoulders are little and afraid.

For many days I do not cut and I do not carve. I do not sweep the cutting room. I do not listen to the sisters when they take their coffee. I do not and do not. And I am not sleeping. It is still summer but it is late summer. It is late summer and it feels late. It is almost too late to sit on the hill in the main part of Rose Head. With the smell of the sun on the grass. To be in the chapelhouse at night with the windows open. I listen. The crickets are loud in late summer. They know it is almost too late. And near me is the keeper. Who sleeps sitting up in the old chair. I go over the things I can do to leave. There are things. The diamond saw is no good. It needs the plug. But there is the hammer and the chisel. And there is the handsaw. It is not easy to break doors or windows with these tools. But people. People break with them. It takes putting the hammer and chisel under my apron. Then at night going into Rita's room first. Then Rosmarge's. If it is the hammer and chisel it has to be their skulls. If it is the saw it has to be their necks. There is blood either way. There has to be. The hammer and chisel and their skulls. I think that is the right way. I get up from the long couch in the side room and start my work again. When I look at Rita I am thinking about where to put the chisel. Behind her ear. Yes, I think so. When I look at Rosmarge it is hard. I think I have only one hit from the hammer with Rosmarge. Maybe not her skull. I think her neck is the place. The chisel in the small circle of her throat. One hit. But there is so much dust in her throat. The sisters use cement dust when my wrist is bleeding. It stops the blood. If I use the hammer and chisel on Rosmarge's throat and the cement in her closes the hole as soon as I can make it and she is fine. That is what I am afraid of. It is her forehead where I put the chisel. Each time she looks up at me from her work bench I see the chisel. I see my hand bring the hammer down hard. I see myself saying to Rosmarge, Peace be thine. The chisel is in the center of her forehead. My hand is bringing the hammer down. Peace be thine, Rosmarge.

Cutting the slate is loud. So loud I cannot think. I cannot think of Rita's skull or Rosmarge's forehead. Or the chisel and the hammer. Cutting is a rest. The loudness is a rest. And I have to wear the face mask when I am cutting. It is better when the sisters cannot see my face. Carving is not as loud as cutting. So I would rather cut but Rosmarge has me carve. It is her eyes. They are scratched and cannot see to carve well anymore. She can still cut. She can cut blind she says. I surprise the sisters at how good I carve. Neither of my hands is as good as Rosmarge's. My lines bend a little. Rosmarge thinks the S's are strangled. The O's boxy. I make mistakes in the cutting room and the quarryman brings extra slate. Still the sisters think I have cutting and carving in me. But I also have other things in me. Planted in me. It is very like the keeper to plant a particular flower at a particular stone. He does not say his reasons. One of the Touissant family dies. This Touissant wants a white pine sapling planted at his grave. The family does not agree. The Touissants are from the north where columbine grows along the roads. All of them have purple columbine at their graves. The keeper plants columbine for this new dead Touissant. But it is not purple. It is blue and on foggy mornings this columbine is the color of white pine. My hands are full of thoughts. It is too loud in here for a head to think. My hands are the things thinking. The fingers from one hand touch a finger on the other hand. They pull the finger and rub it. That is thinking. It is hard to think with a head here. It is the noise and also the cold. The cold makes the noise from the tools louder. The cold holds the noise and then later lets it go. Louder. It is August and it is so cold in here. Sometimes the cold holds the noises for hours. Even at night when the cutting room is locked I am hearing the tools hitting the stone. And when it is quiet again I am seeing the chisel on Rosmarge's forehead.

I do not like thinking about the bindweed night. My last at Rose Head. But now I have to. It is my wrist. Something is happening with it. And now I have to think. That night bursts open and it is as long as a field. A long field of brown grass and goldenrod. My hand goes to pick one thought. How I want the keeper to see the bindweed on the burnpile the next morning and to think I am a good groundskeeper and let me stay. No. How the tubers looked like the keeper's fingers and I put them in me. And the dirt in Pearl's grave and how warm it is. No. Who found me at Pearl's grave and in what way. *Upon thine arm.* The thoughts blow away. *He didn't get her.* The field goes bare. It is cement now. That is what it is like when I think about that night and I have to now. There are bones loose in the dirt at Pearl's grave. Her body is not in a box like the others. It is still dark out. I am feeling for bindweed. For its shoots and tubers. One tuber leads to another. I pull. I pull it right up. But it is light and dead and not attached to anything. It feels empty. An old taproot. No. It is a bone. Pearl's wrist bone. My thumb is on Pearl's wrist bone. A bone is dead. But this wrist bone at Pearl's grave is not dead. It is like a crocus bulb that sleeps all winter then wakes. And now it is awake. My wrist is cut on a shard of curved glass in the dirt. I don't see that the cut is deep and I keep weeding. Keep pulling up bindweed roots. Then I pull Pearl's wrist bone up from the dirt. And after I pull it up, I put my own wrist back into the dirt. To keep digging. I put my own wrist back in the grave. And it stays. This is the problem. My wrist is not here at Marguerite Concrete. It is Pearl's wrist that is here. Yes I am good at the cutting and carving. I am very good at it. The sisters say it is in my blood. They are feeling surprised at how fast I am learning the trade. But then there is yesterday. The day is done. It is time to stop working and Rosmarge is about to lock the cutting room. I am taking the chisel and hiding it under my apron. I am taking the hammer. I take the chisel in my right hand. It drops. I pick it up. I am trying to hide the chisel in my pocket. It drops again. My right wrist is moving itself in crooked ways. Because it is not mine. I pick up the hammer. It is heavier and harder to drop. My fingers curl around the handle but the wrist flings the hand back. I drop the hammer and it makes a loud sound on the cutting room floor. And there is Rosmarge. Looking at me. I pick up the hammer again try to put it beneath my apron. My wrist goes crooked. Even Rita hears it fall. She says to Rosmarge, What is she doing? Rosmarge looks at me and laughs with her eyes and coughs with her mouth. Then she looks at Rita. This one's hell bent on getting out. I can see the chisel on her forehead. *In silence there to rest.* I pick up the chisel but Pearl's wrist makes me drop it again.

Pearl's wrist lets me try to leave but it does not let me hurt the sisters. For a little while I want to see what Pearl's wrist does and does not do. I pick up the chisel and think of Rosmarge's forehead. Pearl's wrist drops it. I pick up the chisel with my other hand and see it next to Rita's ear. Pearl's wrist grabs it. And her wrist also listens. There are certain times when I am working when Pearl's wrist stops the work. It wants to listen. A bereaved comes to the door and talks about the stone they want. And sometimes the box for the body. Or the clothes for the body. Rita talks back to them. Rita really is the nice one. She cries her stones with the bereaved. Some stand at the door and talk for a long time. Rita wraps herself in the Chantilly and talks back and Rosmarge comes coughing in from the back. It is when a bereaved talks about the embalmer that Pearl's wrist stops to listen. Some of the bereaved do not mention the embalmer. Some of them do not say that they are going there. Or that they have just been there. Some of the bereaved seem to know what Rita and Rosmarge do if they hear *the embalmer.* If someone says *the embalmer* Rita turns to stone. Her lips are apart. The way that lips open a little to say a word. But no sound comes. And her lips do not close. Rita turns to stone. If Rosmarge is also at the door it is different. Rosmarge is like stone every day. She has stone inside of her. When she coughs it sounds like stone grinding against bone. Her rib bones have a stone that is scraping and cutting them. She is hard. Her face is hard and her skin. When my wrist is bleeding my first days here she holds it very hard. And she talks in a hard way. If the quarryman is late with the slate Rosmarge will say, That one's taking his time. And Rita will say in a soft way, Oh. Oh is Rita's way of not agreeing. Rosmarge doesn't like Rita's *Oh*. Not for the disagreement but for the softness. Or if Rita and Rosmarge know the dead whose stone is being cut, Rita says, This one's a shame. And Rosmarge coughs. When she agrees she coughs. If she doesn't agree she says, Certainly is. Her voice hard. Certainly is. But if the bereaved says *the embalmer* and Rosmarge is at the door it is different. She gets so hard she breaks. She breaks into dust. She says, Him. He. And she is so hard when she says it that she breaks. *Him* or *He* comes out of her mouth as dust. It is a small wind of dust blowing out of her body. The sisters do not say *the embalmer*. Whose name is Viti. Pearl's wrist unplugs the saw or stops the hammer or hose when the bereaved say *embalmer* or *Viti*. Some of the bereaved say that. They say, I've just been to Viti's. And Rita turns to stone and Rosmarge's stone breaks and I hear it. I do not ever hear the sisters say *the embalmer*. But now I am hearing them not say it.

There are Vitis buried at Rose Head. There is a plot for the Viti family. They have daisies there. The shasta daisies. Which do not need keepers. They grow by themselves and return every year and have a bad smell. Like something dead. Some in Little Neck know the sisters well enough to not say the embalmer's name. The carpenter comes by to talk. Or the quarryman or his daughter. They never say *Viti*. Some of the bereaved do. Because they don't know the sisters. Or because they do and they want to see what the sisters say when they hear the name. Some of the bereaved say, Going to embalmer's next. Or, Just come from up the street. And they nod north, where the embalmer's is. When they say it, they say it quickly. Or they say it and look right at Rita. They look at her like they want her to say, I'm sorry. They want her to be sorry but not for them. They look at her like they want her to say sorry for something she did. And Rita nods and looks straight back at them. Or they say *Viti* or *the embalmer* when Rosmarge is there. Then she looks at Rita. But Rita does not look at Rosmarge. Some bereaved say *Viti* to see what the sisters do. And then Rita is smarter than Rosmarge. If a bereaved says *Viti* then Rita smiles. Her skin is dusty and very dry. When she smiles her cheeks crumble. With the stones crying from her eyes and her cheeks crumbling what she looks like is old concrete. Bad concrete. And then the bereaved don't know what to say. It is over. But Rosmarge is not smart about it. If someone says *Viti* then Rosmarge says Him. He. The bereaved say, I've just been to Viti's with clothes for the body. Or, Viti says he'll take good care of the body. And Rosmarge says, How about that. She says it with a lot of air. As if she doesn't care. The way she usually talks is heavy. There is a gravestone in her throat. The gravestone gives her air only a little bit of room to escape her body. When she tries to talk with a lot of air her voice is small. And it is a mistake to use a small voice when saying *How about that*. Either the bereaved don't know that they should not say Viti and so they take *How about that* to mean that Rosmarge wants to hear about the embalmer. Or they hear how small her voice is and look at her like she is small. One old woman says it. *Viti*. She knows what she is saying. And Rosmarge's voice comes out small. And then the old woman breathes in a lot of air. She breathes in like the air is going to make her bigger than Rosmarge. And then she opens her mouth. She is saying something. It's a pity. That is the first thing she says. It's a pity. There is more. Pearl's wrist wants to listen. But Rosmarge closes the door on the old woman and says *It's a pity* in a terrible way for many days. Then there is the day that a bereaved says, Just come from Viti's. It is another old woman. A lot of the old women in Little Neck seem to know the sisters. Or about them. She says, Just come from Viti's. I am moving a piece of slate from the back room to the cutting room. My hands are on the slate. Pearl's wrist on the right. Mine on the left. When the woman says *Viti's* Pearl wrist drops her side of the slate. My hand can't hold it alone. It breaks on the stone floor. Into four pieces. Rosmarge and Rita hear it drop. They walk in and look at my face. That is something they do not do. They look at my shoulder. Rosmarge looks at my wrists and hands. If I am doing something she does not like she looks at my mouth. When I walk by the sisters they look where I am walking. It does not feel that I have a face for them to see. Then the slate drops and breaks into four pieces and they look right at it. My face.

Or Pearl's wrist puts down the tools and wants me to go closer to the front room. Today it is the quarryman's daughter at the door. She likes to come talk with Rita and Rosmarge. And she has one hand. Her other hand was cut off at the wrist and the sisters like to talk about it when she leaves. Rita will say, Poor thing. And Rosmarge will say, You think. And that will get Rita started on how the quarryman's daughter loses her hand. It is a story she likes to tell. The quarryman's daughter is playing far down in the quarry. Rocks move. Her hand gets stuck. Her people can't find her. But the kids in Little Neck know she must be in the quarry. In the old part that gets filled with rain. They are not supposed to play there but they do. None of them says a word. They think the quarryman's daughter is drowned. Rita says, We all go to bed that night thinking she is gone. It is three days before the town finds her. Her father has all the tools and moves the rock easily. But her hand is dead. They have to cut it off at the wrist. That is years ago. And she can't learn her father's trade. After the quarryman's daughter leaves Rita and Rosmarge like to go over the story but today she leaves and Rita doesn't say, Poor thing. Instead she says to Rosmarge, Remember when you and her—. And Rosmarge right away says, Yes. And Rita says, And then Father was so—. And Rosmarge right away again says, Yes. And then she says to Rita, Don't call him that. And Rita doesn't say anything. Then she says, I forgot. For one minute I forgot. And Rosmarge says, You forgot. And she laughs. It is a horrible laugh and the gravestone in her throat is shaking. Rita and Rosmarge sit by the door a long time. I'm in the front room listening. And then Rita says, You heard he's—. Then she doesn't say anything. Rosmarge says, What. Then again. *What.* Rita doesn't say anything else.

Pearl's wrist is doing things. Pearl's wrist is not the shape my dreams take thereafter. Hereafter. In the stonehouse. No. Her wrist is starting to carve its own words. A bereaved wants *Freed from this body*. It is an epitaph for someone who is sick a long time before he dies. And Rita says, Certainly. In a kind way. Rosmarge says nothing. I can see she likes that epitaph. After the door closes Rosmarge says it out loud. *Freed from this body.* Then she coughs. And Rita laughs. And then they are both laughing and coughing. I put the facemask on. I don't want to have scratched eyes and dusty throat. Like the sisters. I am working on the *Freed*. The cursive *F* is hard. *F* is nearly as hard as an *S*. There is a way to hold the hammer and the chisel to make the round parts. It's the wrists that do the work. My left wrist holds the chisel and Pearl's wrist holds the hammer. But also there is a feeling the carver has to have. Rosmarge calls it *a bent*. The carver has to have *a bent*. But to myself I say *sweep*. To carve the round parts of each letter I need a certain feeling. To make the round parts I need a sweep. I pick a small time with the keeper. It has to be the smallest time I can think of. I pick the time I am opening the door of the chapelhouse. It is early in the summer of the trouble. The day is bright. I can't see into the chapelhouse screen door. I am going in. Hand on the knob. And the keeper's hand is on the inside knob. He is beginning to push the door open to come out. Oh, he says. His eyelids go up. He is looking at me. And then he is not. I am still looking at him. His beard is cut. His chin hairs are shorter. His chin hairs must feel the way grass does in dry months. My hand holds the doorknob. My mouth stays closed. *All flesh is grass.* Then he goes out and I go in. It is a small short time. It is a small thought but it sweeps my hands. I do not stop looking at this small picture in my head. Of the keeper looking at me in the doorway. And that is the mistake. My eyes are not watching my hands carve. My eyes are at Rose Head. It is the summer of the trouble. The sun is bleaching the graves on the hill. The grass goes yellow. And then my tongue is going into the grass. The carver needs to make the curved part of the F. The sweep. I have a very good sweep. I do not stop thinking. I need to stop but I do not. My eyes are watching my hand move across the hill. Hairs from the keeper's chest come curling out of the dirt. They are soft and smell like grass. I put my nose and mouth right in the hairs. The ridge of the hill is the keeper's arm and my head is on it and my arms go around the hill. The dust of Marguerite Concrete is gone from my nose. The sweat on his neck and upper lip smells like winter. Not like cold air but wet air. The wet air in winter. There is mushroom sweat coming from his pants. Dark sweat that smells of the mushrooms coming up near the back wall after rain. And then I start to dig. I am digging a tunnel through the keeper's chest. I have to break his skin with my teeth. Dirt is running out of his chest. It is dirt inside the keeper and not blood. What a long hill the keeper is. I dig and dig. With my mouth. His chest goes on forever. I'm thirsty and taking breaks to drink the wet air sweat from his upper lip. And then I hit a rib. My mouth has struck bone. Or I think at first it is bone. But it is tree root. Now I am inside the chest tunnel. The keeper breathes and the hillside moves. It is warm here inside the keeper. I keep digging. But then I fall through him. I have dug into a hollow part of the hill. Dug right down through the hillside into Rose Tomb. It is the biggest tomb at Rose Head. It is where the keeper sleeps on the hottest days. Inside the tomb on an empty stone slab. I fall into Rose Tomb and there is the keeper's body on the slab. I look up. It is not the tomb. It is Marguerite Concrete and I am on my knees and I am making the sweeping feeling that carvers need. There is the *F* on the stone before me. But Pearl's wrist is not making an *R* and not making an *E*. While I am thinking Pearl is making an *A*. Then a *T.* I make the *F* and Pearl makes the *A* and the *T* while I am thinking. Then I watch her wrist make *H. E. R. He didn't get her.* The sisters are in the front room by the door but Rosmarge hears the chisel. It is Pearl's wrist. She is making the hand hold the chisel too tightly. Rosmarge can hear when a hand holds the chisel too tightly. And she can hear when the carving is going too fast. She comes in and reads the stone with her scratched eyes. It does not say *Freed from this body*. It says *Father*. Rosmarge picks up the stone. It is heavy. She lifts it as high as her chin and throws it down. It cracks only a little. She opens the cellar door and throws the stone down the cellar stairs. Rita is pulling at her Chantilly. She doesn't know what is happening. Rosmarge is not this strong. She has to use the cart to bring the stones from room to room. Rosmarge is picking up this stone and lifting it up to her chin. Then she throws it down the cellar stairs. Rita and I are listening. Rita goes halfway down the cellar stairs and looks at the pieces so she can read what they say. Now she has her arm around Rosmarge and Rosmarge is coughing and coughing. When the cough stops she says to Rita, Don't call him that.

That night I hear the sisters lock their bedroom doors. The next morning there are two Chantillys. One for Rita and one for Rosmarge. They are taking their coffee in the front room. And in the cutting room there is only one face mask and one pair of gloves. There she is. The carver. That is what Rosmarge says in the morning to me. I go into the front room. The sisters stand up and come close. Rosmarge says, Let's see your hands. Rita stands behind Rosmarge. She is looking at me in a strange way. My hands are out. Rosmarge looks at my hands and at my wrists. She is not laughing and not coughing. She is seeing the blood under my skin. That is the way she is looking at me. She takes the wrist on me that is Pearl's. It is not really my wrist. My wrist is still at Rose Head. In Pearl's grave. My wrist is in the dirt there. And digging down. Into the Rose Head underneath the cemetery. The dirt underneath the dead. When I am little I think underneath the dirt is a pond. A green salt pond and all the dead are swimming in it. Now I think it is a pond made of blood. The blood of all the dead in the town. All the blood the embalmer takes from the bodies goes down into that pond. And my wrist is trying to get to it. But Pearl's wrist is here at Marguerite Concrete. And it is also digging. Digging at Rita and Rosmarge. I know her wrist wants to dig at the sisters. And they know it too. But I am curious why Pearl's wrist wants to do this. The sisters say to each other my first night at Marguerite Concrete. *Pearl continues to surprise.* They know their sister well. She hath not yet done all she could. Rosmarge has Pearl's wrist in her hands. She presses hard into the scar. She is feeling for Pearl. The scar is alive and smooth. It feels like a stem or root. On the bindweed night I do not know the cut on my wrist is so deep. The dirt feels good. The grave is dark. *The night shineth as the day*. I am going to make the keeper see that I am a good groundskeeper. He says that come winter I have to go. To Marguerite Concrete. He says no more. *The night shineth as the day*. That is the epitaph on a Jaroslav grave. It is an old stone. Carved before Rosmarge is ever born. It is on the east cape of Rose Head close to the sea. In that part of the cemetery the wind blows the words out of the stones. I have to use my fingers to read the words. The keeper says, Come winter... This is after what happens at the Peggy gravestone. It is only August when I wake up here. And I am not wearing my nightclothes. I am wearing them when I go to Pearl's grave to dig the bindweed and then I am not wearing them at Marguerite Concrete. I don't know if the sisters take them off me or if the keeper does. I am bleeding and the keeper uses the clothes to stop the bleeding and then throws them on the burn pile. No. The keeper carries me to the chapelhouse. He lays me out on the table. And he dresses me like the embalmer dresses the dead. The air is full of water and his fingertips are alive and smooth. Mushroom stems. When I wake up at Marguerite Concrete my skin is damp. No. The air that night is full of salt and his fingertips are dead and rough. When I wake up at Marguerite Concrete my skin is dry. And the keeper buries my bloody nightclothes in his drawer. Rosmarge has Pearl's wrist in her hand. When the sisters get very close to me I can smell them. Their smell is dust.

The quarryman's daughter is back to talk with the sisters. Now Rita and Rosmarge are both answering the door. They like it this way. Today my hands have nothing to do. Nothing to cut. It is almost winter again. *Time doth settle.* I bring my hands to the peonies growing from my chest. Two peonies where the breasts would be. They start in the spring before the summer of the trouble. They are well rooted. They like the cold of the stone house. They bloom all year here. The cold keeps them. Their smell is light and green. I like to hold them and to smell them. The keeper likes to put his whole hand around each flower. His hand around the neck of a columbine. His whole hand around a patch of forget-me-nots. He does it with the peonies at Rose Head. When they are tight green fists. His hand is the blanket and he is warming them. Later they are so heavy they cannot stand up. His hand is the cup and he is drinking them. Or his whole hand around a lilac. His skin is red and very warm. His fingers never touch a thing. My fingers are on the petals. My hands have nothing to cut. I am listening to the sisters. They talk about people in Little Neck. But they do not talk about the keeper. Not since my first night here. On the first night the sisters want to talk about the keeper. They know him. They know him and want to talk about him. But they are not going to say what they know. What is it that you call him. That is what they ask. He takes good care of you now doesn't he. Saying and not saying. The room is so cold even though it is August. Don't have a lot of visitors over at the chapelhouse do you. Going to miss him aren't you. It is a room of no salt. No dirt. No birds. I close my eyes. When she thinks I am asleep Rosmarge says, She is a quiet one though. And Rita says, Just like Peter. And Rosmarge says nothing. Or she does but it takes her a long time and I am asleep. On that night they seem to love to talk about him. And then not. None of the bereaved talks about the keeper. They come to the stonehouse and they talk to Rita about what they have to do for their dead. They say, Going down to Rose Head. But they don't say keeper. Or groundskeeper. I do not hear the sisters or the bereaved ever talk about the keeper. Which means there is something to say. I go stand behind the open door to the front room. Now I can hear the sisters and the quarryman's daughter. They are talking about the Rose family. Someone in the Rose family is dying. The quarryman's daughter likes to talk about the Rose family because they have big houses. The biggest in Little Neck. The quarryman's daughter does not ever say *the keeper*. And I do not hear her say the name *Peggy*. The name on a gravestone at Rose Head where the keeper's favorite flowers are planted. None of the bereaved in Little Neck say the name *Peggy* when they come to the stonehouse. I do not ever hear that name. That gravestone has one name. And dates. And an epitaph. *In sorrow across eternity.* It is Rosmarge's work. Now that I am at Marguerite Concrete I know it is Rosmarge who carves that epitaph. And no last name. The stone is at the bottom of the hill in the cemetery's main part. It is one of only two places at Rose Head with white peonies. The keeper's favorite. He waits for them. When they open in June it means summer is here. All the rest of the year summer is coming. That is something the keeper says. Not loud. To himself. The words stay in his mouth. *Summer is coming. Coming in.* The keeper's voice is quiet and it sounds like he has dirt in his throat. I hear him every spring of my life say it. *Summer is coming.* I love how the keeper says it. All the words die in his mouth.

The best time to say a word is in the morning when the sisters are having their coffee. I do not talk at Marguerite Concrete. I do not talk to the sisters at all. I nod. Or not. I listen. It is easy not to talk. And today when I say the word it is going to be a surprise for the sisters. *Peggy*. I am going to say that name. Today is a talking day. A questions day. Peggy's gravestone. The person choosing the epitaph for her. The person choosing the flowers for her grave. Rita is very good at talking to the bereaved. She is the nicer sister. When the bereaved knock on the door it is Rita they are knocking for. She helps them with the stone. And she helps them with other decisions. With the carpenter. With the gathering. She does not help them with the embalmer and no one asks. But if a bereaved wants something they tell Rita. Then Rita tells Rosmarge. And if Rosmarge asks for something it is done. The bereaved of someone named Peggy tell Rita *white peony*. She says *white peony* to Rosmarge. There are going to be white peonies. The word gets to the keeper. But who sends that word about the Peggy grave. There are family names at Rose Head. Jaroslavs. Roses. O'Keefes. Padulas. The dead's people put the family name on the stone. Or the first name and the family name. Sometimes the dead's people ask for flowers. The Touissants choose columbine. The Jaroslavs choose lupine. Blue lupine. The wind takes their seeds down into the paupers' part. There are no names in the paupers' part but there is blue lupine along its sand road. The keeper's favorite flower is white peony. There are only two places at Rose Head with white peony. One is Peggy's grave and one is me. I think with my fingers and sleep with my eyes. My mouth is closed and ready to make the *P*. I am in the doorway of the side-room and waiting for the sisters to look at me. Their eyes are small and old. When I see their eyes I see crabapples on the sand road. The apples sitting in the sun. Getting smaller and blacker. The sisters do not know that I am about to talk. To make the *P* in Peggy the lips start closed. The face is at rest like the dead. I don't need to breathe in or out to start the name. The lips look wired shut. Shut by the embalmer. My lips are closed and I do not speak at Marguerite Concrete. My lips are together and now they are opening and the air is about to push out. And then there is a hand in front of my mouth. The wrist on me that is Pearl's wrist has put my hand over my mouth. All my air is staying in. The surprise is for me. Rosmarge is not the smartest sister. It is Pearl. She is the smartest one. *And the righteous shall shine forth as the sun.* That is an epitaph that Rosmarge hates. *And the righteous shall shine forth.* I stand before the sisters. My hand is over my mouth. The skin on it smells like the salt marsh. Was she about to talk. That is what Rita says to Rosmarge. Was she about to talk. Rita says to me, What. What is it. My hand is still over my mouth. There is the sound of a truck outside the stonehouse. It is the slate delivery. Rita says to me, Oh. Yes. We hear it. Rosmarge opens and closes her crabapple eyes.

It is about to be busy. It is winter again and the sisters say the dead are coming. There are going to be a lot of dead very soon. It is the way with winter they say. The days are shorter and darker and easier to die in. It is about to be busy. But right now there is a lull. In the lull I am making my plans. My plans are to know about Peggy. And the white peonies at her grave. To know that and then to leave Marguerite Concrete. I am taller now. I want the keeper to see. He does not come to the Marguerite Concrete door. I have to go back to him. I have to go back before I am like the sisters. They have stonecutter hands. The skin on their hands is almost as silver as the tools. It looks sick. It is dry. And covered in dust. And in yellow crusts. The chisel slips. Or the saw. Their skin breaks. No blood comes out. The blood doesn't run in their bodies fast enough to come out before the skin crusts. It makes a yellow crust. And the slate dust is over everything. Their hands are a sick silver. Or not sick silver but cement. The color of cement. When the chisel slips on my skin there is still blood. A bereaved comes to the door of the stone house. Rosmarge has the hose going. The sisters still like to use the hose. They wash down the dust two times a day. So they do not hear the knocking. I do not want to yell for Rita. Like Rosmarge does. I am not one of the sisters. More knocking. I am at the door. It sounds like the knock of someone who does not want to make noise. Which is the way the keeper knocks. It is the keeper's knuckles making this sound. The keeper is here. I cannot open the door. Rosmarge locks it from the inside. But I can see myself opening the door and seeing the keeper. Here. *Till in Death we take our place.* The fresh air is hitting my eyes and my eyes are crying stones and the keeper is here. He is putting his hand beneath my chin as a bowl to catch the stones. His hand is a bowl of small stones. He empties it onto the dirt outside the door. And then he says of the dirt, Huh... Rocky. Yes that's what he says. Huh... Rocky. He says that a lot when he is digging a gravesite. But it is too much to hear him say it now. It is too much and I close the door. The keeper is gone. No he is here. *Till in Death we take our place.* The door opens out. Sometimes the bereaved shiver when the door opens out because it pushes the cold of the stonehouse onto their skin. But the keeper does not shiver. The keeper is here at the door. I feel my peonies opening. My blood feeds them and the cold keeps them. They are wide open and the air around my chest and neck holds their smell. When the door opens the peony smell goes out. The petals full and wide open and breathing. The keeper leans in to smell with his mouth. We are both in the doorway. Across from me the keeper is breathing. And we stand for a long time. Waiting. But for nothing. It is a summer feeling to wait for nothing. To wait for what is already there. To wait inside of what you want. It is the keeper's breath that the peonies want. The keeper breathes. I close the door. Knocking. A bereaved is knocking. The door is locked. Rita finally hears it. I am made to go back to the cutting room. She opens the door. It is not the keeper. He has not come to Marguerite Concrete. No. He is waiting for me at Rose Head. *Till in Death we take our place.* There is a lull and I am making my plans. To know why Peggy gets white peonies. And then to go.

Someone in the Rose family is dead. They are the family with the two big houses near the salt marsh. I can see the houses from the east cape of Rose Head. A bereaved from the Rose family has come to talk to the sisters and I am listening from behind the side room door. They are asking for a new inscription. The Rose family do not have gravestones. They have a tomb. Rose Tomb. The carver goes into the tomb and chisels the name of the new dead inside. And the keeper plants rugosa there. Sea roses. My first days at Marguerite Concrete I want the cut on my wrist to bleed and bleed until the blood goes under the door of the stonehouse. And down to Rose Head. A line of my blood half a mile long and the keeper sees it. He leans down and puts his finger in it. Then brings his finger to his mouth. He knows what it is. He knows the taste of my blood. It is not the first time he is tasting it. When the keeper tells me I have to leave Rose Head I say nothing. It is midway in the summer of the trouble. It is after what happens at the Peggy gravestone. He says I have to leave. He says in the winter I have to go work at Marguerite Concrete. He says that. I leave the chapelhouse and go to the hill over the doors of Rose Tomb. To the rugosa bushes. And I bite my knee. I bite off a piece of skin the size of a rose petal. Then I bury that skin beneath the rugosa and the bush takes to my blood. By the next day its flowers are turning darker. Within days they smell like my blood. And by late July the rose hips are not the bright color they should be. The rose hips are as dark as blood. I make a sour tea out of them. For the keeper. And I watch him drink it. He likes rose hip tea. And coneflower tea. In the spring he likes violet tea. The steam from the rose hip tea smells like my blood. He drinks it. The bereaved from the Rose family need a carver to add an inscription inside the tomb. I am listening through the door's crack to Rita say, Of course. Of course. I am listening to Rita writing down the inscription. Rosmarge is there too. Tomorrow, she says to the bereaved. We are doing it tomorrow. To-morrow a carver needs to be at Rose Head. Tomorrow I am going to Rose Head. And seeing the keeper. He is the one who unlocks the tombs. So it is going to be to-morrow. I am saying *tomorrow* to the starving part of me. And then Rosmarge's voice is also talking to me. She is looking at me through the crack in the door. Her eye is close to my eye. Rosmarge is a stonecarver and for stone-carvers words are what you can touch. What you can see. Rosmarge is looking at me through the crack in the door. She sees something on me saying *tomorrow*. She is seeing the word on my face. Rosmarge is there and seeing and laughing. Oh no you don't. I am walking back into the side room. Rosmarge says through the door crack, Look at you thinking you're going on a little trip tomorrow. Her voice gets further away. She is turning back to Rita. This one, she says. And coughs and laughs. That night I trick Pearl's wrist. There is always slate dust on the cold floors of Mar-guerite Concrete. I reach the hand with Pearl's wrist for the broom. I am tricking Pearl. I reach that hand for the broom and then bite it. I have the thumb and part of the palm in my mouth and with one finger on my left hand I am writing in the dust. *Peggy.* Then to the side room. To sleep. All night I listen. The cold in the stonehouse makes the sounds louder. Sometimes the cold is so thick that it holds the sounds in. Then drops them. Sometimes the cold holds the sounds for hours. Then in the middle of the night the cold lets go and we hear the tools drop and the sisters cough and the bereaved knock. The sounds stay in the air. I write *Peggy* with my finger in the dust and then

I listen. The cold might drop a sound from a day a long time ago. A day when the sisters are cutting the gravestone for someone named Peggy. When Rosmarge is starting its epitaph. *In sorrow across eternity.* I wait that night to hear a sound from a long time ago. Waiting is a kind of carving. All that night I am carving time. But the cold does not drop any sounds from a day when Peggy's gravestone is here at Marguerite Concrete. The cold air keeps all its sounds that night. There is no sound at all. I listen all night. There are no old sounds and no nightly sounds. Not even the sound of air trying to get into Rosmarge's throat and then trying to leave again. There is no sound. The cold is holding all sounds in. Or no. Maybe this is the way it is in the days that Peggy dies. No sound at all. Peggy's bereaved come to the door. And what it sounds like is deadness. The quiet of the grave. But even at the grave there are birds. No one tonight is even breathing. Then it is morning. Rita wakes up first. Rosmarge always takes longer. I hear Rita go into Rosmarge's bedroom. I hear them both walk through the cutting room. But they do not stop. They don't see *Peggy* written in the dust. They walk right across the word. Then Rosmarge leaves for Rose Head. She has the tools and she is the carver again for the day. She is the person waiting for the keeper to unlock Rose Tomb. There are not many bodies in Rose Tomb now. The white bugs and the rain leaking in from the hillside turn them to dirt. It does not take long. And Rose Tomb is where the keeper naps in the heat of the day. On the stone slab in the middle. There are no bodies there. It is cold on the Rose Tomb slab even in summer, and the keeper rests there with his bare skin on the cold slab and his shirt on the ground and his head turned one way so that his cheek is on the slab too. Then he wakes and goes back to mowing. It is winter today and Rose Tomb is cold. It is cold like Marguerite Concrete. And Rosmarge is adding the name of a new dead on the back wall of the tomb. And the keeper is there. I try to open the back door of the stonehouse. Rita cannot hear me try. I try the cellar bulkhead. Rita goes to make her coffee and I try the front door. It is also locked. But there is the little notebook that Rita keeps by the door. Where she writes down what the bereaved want. I bite the hand with Pearl's wrist and with my other hand write in the little notebook. *Peggy.* It is bad writing. But big. Even the sisters' scratched eyes can see it.

Rosmarge is at Rose Head. There is a lull and I have nothing to carve. I am stuck in my skull. With the keeper. The keeper loves peonies. But it is only the dark pink ones that he plants at Rose Head. The keeper has bushes of the dark pink peonies along the sunny side of the chapelhouse. There is no place for praying in the chapelhouse. No place for kneeling like how the bereaved do at a grave. Little Neck goes to the embalmer's for praying and kneeling. Then to Rose Head for burying. But I do not think the embalmer comes. I do not think I have ever seen him at Rose Head. I am never close by when the bereaved are there. In the chapelhouse the small room with a bed is my room. It is the room where the dead used to wait for the end of winter. To be buried. And in the big room is a fireplace for winters and the chair where the keeper sleeps.

This is the room where Little Neck prayed. Now the chapelhouse is where the groundskeeper lives. The small room is on its shady side. And the big room is on the sunny side. In summer I can smell the pink peonies through the windows in the big room. In spring the peony eyes push through. The keeper calls the new red tubers *the eyes*. And he takes his knife and cuts three eyes away. Then he plants the half he has cut off. One peony bush turns into two. There are dark pink peony bushes all over Rose Head. But there are only two white ones. One is planted at the gravestone with the name Peggy. And one is planted in me. But I am not born with the peonies. I do not have the white peonies until the summer of the trouble. It is very hot the summer of the trouble. And the flowers do not last. They bloom and die in days that year. First the lilac. Then the lily of the valley. The irises in four days. Crabapple blossoms in two. *Passing through nature to eternity.* Along the sand road in the paupers' part are the crabapple trees. The paupers' part has all the wild things. And the keeper lets most of it grow. He uses clippers only to keep the grass from hiding the graves and he does not use the mower there at all. Not many people come to visit the dead in that part. And if they do they walk the sand road through the middle and then walk through the high grass to the graves. All the air bugs fly up from the grass into the sun. The crabapple blossoms in that part have a rain smell. Like green clouds. They are hard to smell. Too close to the tree or breathe in the air too hard and the smell breaks. It is the summer of the trouble. It is the first day that the crabapple blossoms open and a storm comes. I run down and pick from the ground as many of their pink petals as I can. Wet. Stuck together. At first too wet to smell. But my hands are warm and start to bring the apple smell out of them. Green clouds. Sweet clouds. And the petals are still wet and not hard to swallow. So I do. There is a fluid the embalmer puts in a dead body. To keep it like a body. I put the fluid from my mouth onto the petals. I embalm the petals on my tongue and swallow. *Herein rests.* But then I do not close my mouth. I want the keeper to smell the crabapple breathing out of me. It is the morning after the storm. We are moving the larger fallen branches to the burn pile. I keep my eyes down and my mouth open. He is going to have to put the branch down and walk over. To get closer to the blossom smell he is going to have to put his mouth on mine. He smells things with his mouth. Flowers. Rain. And the petals are embalmed deep in me. When he puts his mouth right on my mouth it is going to be for a long time. To get at the crabapple smell. That is May. The air has the most salt in May. The flowers are making more flesh and the green more green. *All flesh is grass.* Knocking. Rosmarge down at Rose Head. The sisters say that there is is a lull in deaths before the winter dying starts. But there is knocking. Another bereaved. Or Rosmarge. To say she needs help carving in Rose Tomb. Or the keeper is here. Rosmarge tells him that I am tall now and he is coming to see me. His knuckles on the door of Marguerite Concrete. His knuckles that look like hairy flower bulbs. He finds me that night at Pearl's gravestone. I am digging the bindweed and I am bleeding. And he brings me here and never comes back. He thinks I am dead. That I die at Marguerite Concrete after the bind-weed night. No. I have no grave so I am not dead. Knock-ing at the door. It is the keeper to say, Come back. I am going to open the door and bite off four of his knuckles. Then spit the tulip bulb knuckles to the ground. Then I am going to bite the fifth. The thumb knuckle. But not spit it out. No. I am going to chew off the skin and suck on the thumb bone. Knocking. No it is not the keeper. He is someone who knocks only once. And today he is in Rose Tomb with Rosmarge. I can see where he is. I can see what he is doing. *Till in Death we take our place.* His hand un-locks the tomb door. It is a rusty lock. And his hand has dirt in the skin cracks. Like the bindweed hand from the night at Pearl's gravestone. Five tuber fingers with knuck-les and dirt in the cracks. The hand pressing on me from inside. Its palm is the root and its tuber fingers are touch-ing. Its whole hand inside me and reaching up. The tuber fingers inside and climbing. Curling. And knocking. No. It is a bereaved knocking. Rita does not hear. I do not want to yell for her like Rosmarge does. I go into her bedroom and point toward the front door. She is surprised. It is a lull. There are not usually many deaths this time of year. She goes. She is in a rush. She has the keys and the Chan-tilly. She is in a rush and does not look back to make sure I am gone from the room. She opens the door. A bereaved. A woman. The woman looks at me. And there is Rita now in front of me. She is talking to the woman but the woman is looking at me. Rita is asking many questions. She feels in a rush. The woman is looking at me. My face. But she does not look at my face and see anyone. My face is not the face of someone she knows. She only looks. I go back behind the door and listen. I hear Rita say what the bereaved wants as she writes it in her book. Her little book by the door. I hear her open the book and turn to a new page. Past the page where my hand writes *Peggy* in large letters and right to a new one. Rita does not even see the page. The bereaved wants the epitaph *Gone too soon*. It is not an easy one. There are so many O's. The bereaved says, Still a child. She wants a medium stone. She plans to put forget-me-nots by a medium stone. Rita is writing in the book. Now it is the dates. The woman says the dates. Then she says, About the age of that one there. She points to a spot behind Rita. And Rita is surprised. She turns to look. I am no longer there. I am behind the door watching. Rita says, That one where. It is a question. But the bereaved keeps talking. She wants forget-me-nots. They are small flowers that do not hide the stone. She is going to get the forget-me-not seeds after she leaves Marguerite Concrete. Then she is going to see the new keeper about planting the seeds. She has just gone to the embalmer's. And now she is here at the stonehouse to order the stone. And then she is going to get the seeds from a friend. She is repeating her list. The bereaved say the same things over and over. She has just been to the embalmer's. Now she is here. Then she is going to get the seeds to plant by the stone. Then she is going to see the new keeper about the seeds. The embalmer's. Here. Her friend's house for the seeds. Then the new keeper. I wait. This woman is from Little Neck but she does not know Rita. She does not see what happens to Rita's face when she says *embalmer*. And she does not know that no one in Little Neck says *keeper* to the sisters. And that the sisters do not say *keeper* to each other or to me. Not since my first night here. This woman does not remember that it is winter. The dirt is cold and hard. The grass is brown. Her seeds are going to blow right off Rose Head cliff. Some in Little Neck jump off that cliff. That is what the sisters say. Then the water is their grave. *Passing through nature to eternity.* I wait for the bereaved to say *new keeper* again. While I am waiting the grass is growing brown in the paupers' part. The goldenrod is growing brown and the lupine is falling over. The Queen Anne's lace is curling in and making a cup. The flowers are dead and at rest and still standing. I am dead and at rest in the tall grass. I am waiting and I am dead in the grass and another summer comes. The lupine comes up through my skull and the goldenrod come up around my fingerbones. The bereaved does not say *new keeper* again. She leaves and Rita closes the door. And now there is a sound. Not very loud. It is coming from my skull. The way a cicada sound comes from the trees. It is a whine like that. A high sound. Not very loud at first. I think it begins when the bereaved says *new keeper*. I do not notice the sound at first. It is coming from my skull but I am busy. I am sweeping. Then I hear something. A high sound. A squirrel. A squirrel is trapped in the cemetery's rock wall. There is a rock on the squirrel's tail. I need to go to the hill in the main part. It is the oldest wall. That is where I think the squirrel is trapped. There is a lot of moss on that hill. It is because of the shade from the old oaks there. Their shade makes bright green moss. Or no. The sound is coming from the moss and I lay my ear down on it. The whine is louder here. My skull is so heavy it sinks into the moss. Rough moss that curls like hair. I lick each single hair down to its root. The hairs taste good. The moss is deep on this hill. The whine is getting louder. I have dirt in my mouth and hair stuck in my teeth. No the sound is not moss. It is metal scraping concrete. It is the sound of the metal door of Rose Tomb scraping the concrete steps. Its door is closing and locking. Rosmarge is coming back. The door to Marguerite Concrete is opening then closing then locking. The whine is loud and it is in my skull.

The whine in my skull gets louder. The whine starts to talk. And Pearl's wrist gets stronger. I am working. I am working and I am not waiting to ask the sisters about Peggy and I am not waiting for the keeper. I am waiting only for spring and listening to the whine. And Rosmarge is waiting. Today she is standing in a strange way. It is a strange way because she looks like she is waiting but I do not know what she is waiting for. She is watching me and not saying a thing. She is older than Rita. I think it goes Rosmarge then Rita then Pearl. And Rosmarge is smart and is good at waiting. She is a careful carver. She measures the stones many times. She plots each letter. She is smart and careful and her hands are strong. I am cleaning the saw. And cleaning its diamond blade. And cleaning the chisel. And listening to the whine. Pearl's wrist is getting stronger. Pearl is a cutter. A cutter and a carver. The sisters are interested in the shard of glass buried at Pearl's grave. My wrist gets cut by glass there and they think their sister

Pearl dies by cut. Cutting herself. By taking a shard and cutting her wrist and dying with a shard in her hand. And she has no box. She is there in the dirt. The sisters know Pearl and they know she is a cutter but they are not sure what makes Pearl die. The sisters want to know. I can tell. They want to know because they keep not asking. Rosmarge touches the scar on me. She says, Look at this one, cutting herself open with a beer bottle. Rita says back, No, an accident. An accident with a sharp rock. They keep being interested and they keep not saying. I am not like Rita and Rosmarge. I want to know who Peggy is and I try to ask in a plain way. To say *Peggy* and to write *Peggy*. It is Pearl who stops me. Her wrist. But also I am like the sisters. I want to know why the bereaved woman says *new keeper*. The sisters are saying nothing and I am not asking. And now today the whine is very bad. The whine is saying an epitaph very loud in my skull. *As I live so let me sleep.* Over and over. Loud and high. I am touching my hands to my forehead. And Rosmarge sees me. This is what she is waiting for. She says to Rita, This one's sad. The way she says *sad* sounds mean. It sounds mean but it is not. It is Rosmarge. It is the way she talks. *Now go.* That is the epitaph she picks for her sister's grave. This one's sad. But then Rosmarge says, She's missing her friend. And the way she says that word is terrible. She says *friend* but the way she says it shows she means something else. So Rosmarge knows that I heard *new keeper*. And that is what Rosmarge is waiting for. For me to be the bereaved. To say something about the keeper. She watches me touch my hands to my forehead. It is the whine. It is so loud. But Rosmarge is thinking I am the bereaved. Because I know there is a new keeper. Because I am touching my hands to my skull. *She's missing her friend.* Pearl's wrist is holding the chisel. And then the chisel is buried in Rosmarge's arm. I hear Rita breathe in. She is right there behind Rosmarge. But she breathes in so quickly she coughs. And then Rosmarge coughs too. Rita's cough is her surprise but Rosmarge's cough is her laugh. Rosmarge is laughing. The chisel is sticking out of her arm. It is not in her wrist but farther up. The chisel stands up straight in her arm. It is Pearl's wrist that does it. Rosmarge says *friend* in a terrible way. She says *friend* and means something else. Rosmarge says that and she means to unlock me. And she does. But what she sees inside my box isn't me. It is Pearl. Pearl hears *friend* and buries the chisel in Rosmarge's arm. Now Rita is smiling her bad concrete smile. A smile that crumbles. Rita's face has no shape. And Rosmarge is very close to my face. The chisel in her arm. There is a little blood. Only a little. The dust in Rosmarge soaks up her blood. It runs dry not wet. Rosmarge is looking at my face. She does not see what she is looking for on my face. She looks into my skin and into my blood. She is very close when she says, Pearl. I do not say a thing and Pearl in me does not say a thing. Then Rosmarge pulls the chisel out of her skin. The whine is loud. *As I live so let me sleep.* The whine is so loud. I leave the cutting room to go lie on the long couch. I lie on my side. When I lie like this I can smell dirt. Even in Marguerite Concrete. I can smell dirt. And I can feel moss on my face. I am in the shade next to the rock wall in the main part of Rose Head. It is summer. When I am in the shade I can smell the sun. The whine in my skull is very loud and I am lying on my side on the grass. Rose Head's hills go up and down. The grass goes up and down. I can't see the flowers. I can hear the green but I can't see any flowers. It must be raining. It is starting to rain. When it rains Rose Head goes gray. The flowers get heavy and sink into the grass. The flowers go gray. To match the rain. Now the flowers are the color of concrete.

*O*R NO. I AM WRONG. THERE IS KNEELING IN THE chapelhouse at Rose Head. There is praying there. It is the keeper. He is kneeling in the small room. Where I am sleeping on my back like the dead. He is kneeling in front of the bed. This is how it happens. This is how it has to have happened. The peonies in me. I am not born with them. They only start growing from my chest the summer of the trouble. In May. Two white peonies. One each where my breasts would be. Though I do not know their color until they open in summer. And when they open they have a soft smell. Light, tickling. It must be that the keeper goes to the Peggy gravestone. He divides the crown of white peonies growing there. Half the crown stays at the grave. Half is going to get planted in me. It is early spring. It is the spring before the summer of the trouble. The keeper is kneeling in front of Peggy's gravestone. He is dividing the crown of white peonies. They are his favorite flower. He takes half into my room. I am sleeping on my back. Now he is kneeling in front of my bed. So there is kneeling in the chapelhouse. And praying. And it must be that he pushes my legs away. The way he pushes the leaves back before he smells a flower. Then his hand feels the temperature inside. The warmer the ground the farther the crown must be from the surface. He feels the temperature then turns the eyes of the crown so that they are facing up. And he plants the crown far up in me. The eyes facing up toward my skull. It must be that this happens when I am sleeping. And I don't wake up because the keeper's hands are good at digging. He knows how to dig in a light way. And I don't wake up because the keeper is quiet. He never talks when he is planting. He does not talk much to me at all. He swallows his words to me. There are things he wants to say and he does not. He swallows them. The words are seeds and they are growing in him and then one day there is a whole field. It looks like the field in the paupers' part. Tall grass and wildflowers and weeds and vines. A whole field. And he is standing in the middle of it. His words for me.

$\mathcal{R}$OSMARGE IS GOOD AT WAITING. PEARL IS VERY VERY good. And I am good at waiting too.

And now it is my second spring at Marguerite Concrete. The dust inside Rosmarge is turning to stone. At first when Rosmarge talks there is sand in her throat. Now her whole gravestone is in her throat. When she talks a whole gravestone has to move to the side so that her voice can get out. The sisters want to rest more. They are not that old but they are full of dust. There is not a Marguerite Concrete if I am not here. I am the carver now. The sisters want to watch me and to rest. They watch my face and my hands. And my wrist with the scar. They are seeing Pearl. And they are seeing something else. Or someone. They are watching and hardly talking. They take their coffee and they rest and they look at my face. Which is full of leaving. Rose Head is the only thing in my skull. But the sisters keep the doors locked and at night they lock the tools. And Pearl's wrist does not let me hurt the sisters. What I need is to have myself bleed again. Bleed all over the stone house. So much blood that the sisters cannot stop it. All the blood in me is like a spring rain. A light steady rain on the stonehouse floor. *Until the day breaks.* And then a muddy ground. The dust and the blood making a good mud here. And the sisters have to get through the mud to me. And my body is very light now and they can carry me all the way back to Rose Head. And give me to the ground. And I am asleep with the dirt and the grass and the salt in the air. *Until the day breaks.* But I don't know how to make myself bleed that much without cutting tools or a shard of glass. I don't know how and then one day I do. The smell of the peonies on me is not strong. From the nose to the breast is far. I have to use my hands to bring the peonies closer to my nose. One open peony in each palm. I crane my neck to smell the flowers. At night in the side room I listen. The cold holds the sounds of the day and then drops them at night. I listen at night to the sounds of the day before. And I smell the peonies. And have Rose Head in my skull. The summer of the trouble. The peonies taking root and my chest hurting. I find two rocks and push them into the peonies. The pain from the rocks helps the pain from the peony roots. In the early mornings at Rose Head I reach for the rocks. They are cold and wet and I push them as hard as I can against the peonies. Cold rock pushing in. Green peonies pushing out. The peonies want me to make pain for them as they make pain for me. Pain for pain. And then the day breaks. *There will no longer be any mourning or crying or pain. The first things have passed away.* The sisters make sure I am watching them at night when they lock the cutting room door. They put away the diamond blade in a locked cupboard. The sisters also think bleeding is a good way for me to leave. They think it is going to be my wrist. They think I am going to cut my wrist. My scar is thick. There is cement under my skin. But it is easy to cut a little bit of cement. With the diamond blade I can cut off a wrist. I can see the sisters thinking that. I can see the sisters seeing the saw go through the skin and then the bone. I can see the sisters seeing the blood on the cutting room floor. A puddle. Then a pond. Then a sea. Blood flowing down the road to Rose Head. It is better to cut Pearl's wrist. And cut it fast. Then she cannot stop me. Or it is better to cut my neck. No. The wrist. I can see the sisters seeing me cut my wrist. So much blood it runs out the stonehouse and down the road. It arrives at the main gates of Rose Head and floods through. It turns the grass red. The grass up and down the hills is red and dark. The white pines drink it and the knots on their trunks become bite marks. Their bark turns rusty. It is the heat of the day and my blood is hot. It arrives at Rose Head and waters the rugosa. The coneflowers. Snapdragons. Lupine. The bleeding heart flowers love the blood. And the maggots. They are swimming in puddles of my blood. And it is the heat of the day and the keeper is resting in Rose Tomb and it starts to rain inside the tomb. The keeper has a drop of blood in his mouth. At the top of the hill over the tomb the rugosa and its petals are very glad to have more of my blood. The beetles come later and eat the leaves. They taste like my blood and the birds eat the beetles and they have my blood in their gizzards. And my blood gets old and makes scabs on the grass and then the maggots eat the scabs. I give the dirt at Rose Head so much of my blood that it needs a heart. To help steer its blood. And there is a pebble at Pearl's grave. The pebble is in the dirt near Pearl's rib bones. There is a pebble near Pearl's ribs and the dirt at her grave is so full of my blood that it makes the pebble its heart. The pebble the heart. The dirt the skin on Pearl's bones. Pearl hath not done all she could. But it is not going to happen from a cut on my wrist. No. I know how to do it. It is easy. It is spring again. Summer is coming. I am lying on the couch in the side room. Rita is asleep. Rosmarge is asleep. I have a peony in each palm and I am smelling them. And then I am pulling them. Hard. I am pulling them from their roots. The roots are very deep in me. I am pulling the peonies out of my chest and it is true. There is so much blood. I am bleeding and leaving. It is just like the bindweed night. I love the dirt in all weather. When it is hard and dry in winter. And how it smells when there is a cold rain. Blood is coming out of the two holes in the ground of my chest. I am leaving. *Awaken from the dream of life*. And it is too late for Pearl's wrist to do anything. And the sisters are sleeping. I think to give the flowers to the keeper. The cold in the stonehouse keeps the bloom very well. White peonies. His favorite flower. They have a light sweet smell. I am trying to hold the flowers up away from the blood. *Now go*.

THE NIGHT ROSMARGE DIES SHE DOES NOT LOCK THE doors. She goes in her room and dies in her sleep. Each night in the stonehouse I rinse the dust out of my hair with the hose. And in the morning when it is clean I look at it. My hair is long enough to pull far in front of my eyes. And it is turning green. The light inside the stonehouse is not good. Dawn or day or night. It is never good light. My hair is dark. It is the color of dirt. But I can see green strands too. I pull my hair in front of my eyes in the morning until Rosmarge coughs at the door. Good morning. When I am awake the sisters are near me. Since the night of pulling the peonies up from their roots. The night of making two holes in the ground of my chest. Holes that the sisters fill with Marguerite Concrete. Since that night the sisters are near me. Rosmarge coughs, Good morning. And then she yells to Rita, She's up. Then Rita walks in. And the day starts. But this morning Rosmarge does not come. Rita does not come. I am in the side room going under my hair. Into the green. I am going into the pond beneath the dirt at Rose Head. The thing the cemetery has buried. A pond full of the blood of the dead. In the pond the keeper's voice is saying to me, *In sorrow across eternity.* I hear it from far away. He is at Rose Head. I am at Marguerite Concrete. His voice is like a finger. His voice is full of dirt and shaped like a finger. The sounds coming out of his mouth are fingers and the dirt is deep in them. I am going to have to put each one of his fingers in my mouth. To feel his voice. But it is morning. His voice is drying up. Dead fingertips. Dried fingertip skins. They look like old petals. I throw the dead things up in the air and stand on the grass at Rose Head in the dead skin rain. It is morning and the quiet in the stonehouse is wrong. It is a pinching quiet. I put my hair back up on top of my skull and get up. Rita is in Rosmarge's room. Rita is sitting in the chair that Rosmarge usually sleeps in. Rosmarge sleeps in a chair. To help the dust go in and out of her. Sleeping in the bed makes the gravestone in her throat too heavy. But on her last night she goes to sleep in the bed. On her back. On her back the way the dead are. It is her way of saying something. Rosmarge sleeps on her back that night. She knows she is going before morning. And she does not lock the doors. It is cold in Rosmarge's bedroom. I put my hands over my face. My breath smells like August grass. But also it is dusty. The concrete filling the holes in my chest gets in my blood. And I am starving. Something in me is starving. There is a name for what I am starving for. Rita says, She didn't tell me. Rita looks small this morning. But she has the Chantilly wrapped around her. It is morning and no one is at the door and the Chantilly is already wrapped around Rita. Then Rita says, I'm cold. Her hands are pulling at the Chantilly. Rosmarge goes to sleep knowing she is going to die. And Rita wakes up knowing she is going to be bereaved. She puts on the Chantilly to open the door to herself. The door she opens to being bereaved is not the front door. It is Rosmarge's bedroom door. Rosmarge is not coughing or talking or breathing anymore. But she is still here. It takes a very long time to die. Even after the breathing stops. At Rose Head the trees that fall or get the fungus aren't dead until the keeper puts them on the burn pile. Even then there are pieces of tree ash that are still alive. I think it takes a very long time to die. To be done with what you are made for. When the body stops breathing it is just one thing. Rita wants me to leave the room. She wants to be alone with the body. I cannot see Rita without Rosmarge. But I can see Rosmarge without Rita. Rosmarge burying her sister is not hard to picture. But now Rita is the sister who is left and she looks very small. She wants to be alone with the body. Even then I do not think to leave the stonehouse. I leave the room. I am going to lie down. And I do. In the stonehouse I work and I lie down. Soon I have to cut a stone for Rosmarge. My wrist and Pearl's wrist have to cut Rosmarge a slate grave. And then carve her epitaph. But no. Rosmarge has the cement. There is a bag of cement in the backroom for a gravestone of the famous Marguerite Concrete. Rita and Rosmarge are saving the last two bags for themselves. Rita uses a little to stop the blood coming out of the cut on my wrist. And Rosmarge uses some to stop the blood coming out of my chest. I bleed at Pearl's gravestone and wake up at Marguerite Concrete. I think that if I am bleeding at Marguerite Concrete I will die and wake up at Rose Head. *Awaken from this dream of life.* But I wake up again at Marguerite Concrete. In the stonehouse. Where it is cold and the sisters are watching me and concrete peonies are growing from my chest. Rosmarge makes flowers not breasts. Two small gray fists. I sit up. They are heavier than the real peonies. And they smell like dust. But the real peonies are still in the room. Two white peonies. The keeper's favorite. They are here in a vase. The bottom of their stems is the color of blood. The water they are in is bloody. The bloody water in the vase is the only thing in Marguerite Concrete that is not the color of cement.

It is Rita who knows how to make concrete. Who knows what to mix with the cement. And how. Rita is going to make Rosmarge's stone. Rosmarge is going to have the famous Marguerite Concrete for her gravestone. Then there is going to be only one bag of cement left. For Rita. I do not know who is going to make Rita's stone. I do not know if Rita is the one carving the epitaph on Rosmarge's stone too. I can carve slate very well. Slate is smooth. It breaks or it doesn't. Rosmarge says anyone can carve in slate. Then she says, But now concrete... And laughs. Rosmarge has a laugh that is worse than crying. It is a cough. It has to be Rita who carves the concrete. I am a good carver but I do not know concrete. Or what to carve on Rosmarge's stone. I can see Rita carving *Rosmarge* and no family name. Like on Pearl's stone. Rosmarge has an *O* and an *S*. It needs the feeling. The sweeping feeling. It is hard to think of Rita having the feeling in her wrist. If she can even carve. When Rosmarge is carving an *S* her wrist has a very good sweep. What Rosmarge uses to help her make her sweep is her secrets. She loves not saying things. She loves not saying things about her sisters. Rita. Pearl. The three sisters. Rosmarge, Rita, Pearl. Or not saying things about the father. Viti. Up the road north. That is the direction the bereaved point. Rose Head is the other way. The three sisters. The father. And then there is Peggy. I don't know if Peggy is a sister. But she is something. Her grave does not have a family name. Just a first name. Which is like Pearl's grave. But Peggy's grave has an epitaph that does not sound like Rosmarge. *In sorrow across eternity.* And it has the keeper's favorite flower planted there. One of only two places in the cemetery that has white peonies. No. Now the only place. And when I try to say *Peggy* it is Pearl's wrist that stops me. Rita wants to be alone with the body. I go lie down. I lie down all the time and go into the green. *Awaken from this dream of life.* The quiet in the stonehouse pinches today. But then I hear coughing. Rosmarge is coughing. She is not dead. She is awake and coughing. No. It is knocking. Rosmarge is dead and someone is knocking. A knock that sounds like a cough. I go into the front room. The knocking is louder here. I am at the door. My blood is trying to get out of my skin. Rosmarge always locks the door. And last night she does not. I put my hand on the knob and it turns. The door opens all the way. The sun is late summer sun. It is hot. The air is heavy. Sand is all around the stonehouse. Sand is all there is. And broken slate. Pieces of old concrete. A low concrete wall all around the sand yard. One hydrangea and the quarryman's daughter. Her knock is strong. It is because she has only one hand. The one hand is very strong. She is here to talk with the sisters. She loves to talk. But now she is not talking. She is looking at my face. She is surprised to see me. I am not allowed to answer the door. I wear the cutting room facemask when the bereaved are here. And now I am at the door. With my face. And she sees it. I am not sure I have a face for anyone to see. The keeper does not look at my face. The sisters do not. But now the quarryman's daughter is looking at my face. And she sees someone. The face she is seeing on my face is someone else. This is the first time she is seeing my face. But she is looking at me as if she knows me. It is August. The air is heavy. I can hear the green. And the quarryman's daughter has very small eyes. Like the sisters. Or no. Her eyes are small because she is surprised. She sees a face in my face. She says nothing. And then she says, You have your mother's face. I am in the doorway to outside and it is summer. She says, I know exactly who you are. You have your mother's face. Then Rita is there. And the quarryman's daughter is past me and standing beside Rita. She has only one full arm and it is around Rita. Her arm is around Rita and she says, Can you believe how much she looks like Peggy. Exactly like Peggy. The quarryman's daughter stops. She is saying something she is not supposed to say. She takes her one hand and covers more of Rita with the Chantilly. She does not look at my face anymore. She looks at the Chantilly but talks to me. She says, We knew you were one of them. We knew you must belong to one of his girls. And now the quarryman's daughter looks at Rita's face. Rita's cheeks have a good shape. They are not crumbling. The quarryman's daughter says to Rita, We knew. We knew that was no orphan. We all knew how much he loved his girls. Peter he never got along with. But he loved his girls. A little too much. She is laughing. She is from the quarry and has slate dust in her throat too. It is a coughing laugh. And now she is waving her arm with no hand in the air. A little too much to be sure. And Peggy. Too sweet for her own good. Too good for this life. Now Rita's cheeks are starting their crumble. The quarryman's daughter is saying too much. It is because Rosmarge isn't here. Rosmarge is dead and so the quarryman's daughter can talk like this. But then she stops talking. She is wondering where Rosmarge is. And she makes herself stop laughing. She talks about the weather. She says rain is coming. She says that she feels it coming in her dead elbow. And then I walk out. I am outside and it is summer. And no rain at all. *Rose upon the horizon of a perfect endless day.* There is sand and one hydrangea bush. Its flowers are the color of the lines under the skin on my wrist. And on Pearl's wrist. That color. I am outside. It is summer and day is breaking. It breaks.

Hydrangeas have no smell and they love sick dirt. The sicker the dirt the nicer their color. It would be a good flower to plant by Rosmarge's stone. A flower with no smell. Rita is the bereaved visiting Rosmarge's stone. And there is a flower with no smell for her stonecutter's nose to miss. The hydrangea smells like air. And it gets woody. The branches harden. It needs to be cut back. Rosmarge can hear the handsaw every August from her grave. That is when the keeper cuts back the hydrangea. My body turns in the yard of Marguerite Concrete towards Rose Head. I am going to take a long walk. Day is breaking. Rita is busy taking a bag of cement from the back room and making the famous Marguerite Concrete. Day has broken and it is summer and Rosmarge is dead. Rita is busy and the quarryman's daughter is there to help her. I am taking a long walk. It is summer and the sun is strong. The sun is burning the dust off my hands. And warming the green in my hair. My hair in the sun smells like grass. I am taking a long walk. A long walk and a slow one. My body is turned toward Rose Head. And the tops of the trees on the road are turned towards it. The fist of bindweed inside me uncurls and grows towards it. The toe of my stonecutter's boot kicks a small stone and the stone starts rolling towards Rose Head. The keeper laughs when he sees my stonecutter's boots. His eyes close then open. The lashes on his eyelids touch the skin under his eyes. That is him laughing. There is no sound and his chest does not move. I am taking a long and slow walk to Rose Head. Where the keeper no longer is. But where else can he be. I am following the road. *Thy eternal summer shall not fade.* Every thing this morning is turning toward Rose Head and I am a thing turning toward Rose Head too.

Or the keeper is at Rose Head but he does not have lashes anymore. His eyelashes are falling from his dead skin. Little hairs stick on the bones of his face. The keeper is dead and laughing. He is laughing at my stonecutter's boots.

The little hairs that are on the bones of his face look like the hairs on a raspberry. I am going back to Rose Head. For late August raspberries. There is patch behind the greenhouse. The hairs on the raspberries are the keeper's eyelashes. His hair is moss. His skin the bark. I touch each hair on the raspberry. It takes a long time. Then I eat it. It is the first berry ready on the bush. The keeper's eye and lashes. The keeper is dead and laughing at my stonecutter's boots walking toward Rose Head. The laugh blows his eyelashes into the dirt of his grave. The keeper is standing by the greenhouse. He stands in the raspberry bushes. This is one October. The bees are around the bushes. I know the berry he is going to pick. He likes them very dark. A bruise on the shin. So that they crumble in his hand. He closes his eyes when his fingers put the berry in his mouth. My skull hurts. And my shoulder. That is really where the pain is. My shoulder. I think it is Pearl making the pain. Pearl does not want me to think about the keeper. I am getting very close to Rose Head now. It is only half a mile from the stonehouse. The trees are still bending in its direction. I feel very close to being there. Sap is running up my leg bones. It is almost enough. It is almost enough to almost be there. I am going to lie down in the road in this spot very close to the main gates of Rose Head. In the sun. Almost there. Soon enough. But for Pearl's wrist. Her wrist. My body is turned to Rose Head but Pearl's wrist is turning my hand the other way. To the north. My shoulder hurts because of how strongly she is pointing. Pearl does not want to go back to Rose Head. Or what she wants more is to go the other way. North. Rosmarge is very smart and strong. She keeps Rita from crumbling too much. She keeps Marguerite Concrete locked and me inside. And Pearl locked inside me. Pearl must be the younger sister. Her wrist is strong when Rosmarge is alive. But it is not this strong. Her wrist wants Rita and Rosmarge to know she is there. She digs the chisel into Rosmarge's arm. And she carves *Father* instead of *Freed*. I am turned to Rose Head. Pearl is turning to the north. The street has the morning cool and the sun. With my eyes closed I still have the sun. It is coming in through my lids. The sun looks bloody through my closed eyes. And my breath smells like August grass. The grass around each stone at Rose Head needs to be clipped. I wait for the blade. The bees are working me to sleep. The green is whining in my ears. In winter the algae needs to be scraped from the graves. Something in me is starving for Rose Head. But something else in me is Pearl. Pearl's wrist and hand are turning me north. Pearl's wrist is awake now. A body is not like a bulb. It doesn't wake every year. Only some years. Rosmarge is dead and Pearl's wrist is awake and now I am walking north through Little Neck. I know where Pearl is taking me and I know what she is going to do.

AND THE EMBALMER IS WAITING FOR ME. IT IS Pearl's wrist on my arm that pulls me here and it is Rosmarge who teaches me very well. How to cut and how to carve. It is a big house. It is a big house for a big family. The door is not locked. It opens up into a chapel room. For the bereaved to pray. The embalming room is down the stairs and Pearl's wrist pulls me. He is standing in his embalming room. He says, And there she is. He is talking to no one. Or to himself. And there she is. He is talking and I am in front of him but his talking is not to me. He is smiling. Then he talks to me. Here you are. His teeth are thin and they have sharp points. He is smiling. Calm and smiling. Then he talks to no one again. He says, There she is. The embalmer has almost no bottom lip. And he is waiting. He is not surprised. The smell in the embalming room is very strong. It is a dead smell. Not the smell of the rake pulling away the dead leaves from the rock wall at

Rose Head. The underneath of the leaves is old and wet and it is not a good smell. But it is not that. And it is not the smell of a rat dead near the burn pile. A rat with the white bugs crawling through it. It is a dead smell here but not a smell of something that is alive and then dead. The smell in the embalming room is the smell of something that is always dead. A bad dead. The smell is sweet. A sweet bad dead. And the embalmer is old. He is an old man. He is very gentle and his voice is gentle. A lot of the bereaved like the embalmer. When the bereaved come talk to Rita I can tell they like him. They don't understand why the sisters do not speak to their father. They don't understand why the sisters do not say his name. *Viti.* Or *father.* But the embalmer understands. His voice is gentle and he is an understanding father. And because he is the father something in him knows Rosmarge is dead. He says to me, So she let you out did she. He talks in a way that is just like Rosmarge. Rosmarge is strong. What she says cuts. The embalmer is gentle. But he says things in the same way. Saying and not saying. He says, So she let you out did she. And he says it in a way that makes me know that he knows Rosmarge did not let me out. That he knows Rosmarge is dead. He has a terrible smile and a gentle voice. He does not have any questions in him. He knows why Rosmarge and Rita do not speak to him. Or about him. And his voice is gentle. He is their father. He is not mad. The way he talks makes it seem like the sisters are wrong. Like there is something they do not understand. But he understands. He says, And Rosmarge. And now he makes his voice sad. Rosmarge, she is... I nod. Oh, he says. Very gentle. Oh that's too bad. He says, I have a feeling. A father knows. The embalmer and his teeth are talking so much. He likes to say *You know* in a very gentle way and then tell me something. *You know how it is.* I try to look at him while he is talking. To get his measure. You have to get the measure of the whole stone before you cut. I try looking at his neck. He is all skin. He has the same dried crabapple eyes as Rita and Rosmarge. If the sisters are looking at the embalmer they are seeing their own eyes. They do not have his whole face but they have his eyes. It is easier to look at his smile. At his small and very sharp teeth. But that is where the embalmer wants me to look. At the place where his gentle voice comes out. And you know, he is saying. Very gentle. And you know. There are no embalming tools laid out. There is a shelf with glass bottles. But I do not see any tools for the embalmer to cut. He must keep his embalming tools on his body. He teaches Rosmarge that. Keep your tools close. In the belt. And Rosmarge teaches me. Keep your tools close. But I don't listen. I don't want to be a stonecutter. But now I am one. I cut and I carve. Cutting is in my blood and Rosmarge teaches me very well but I do not have tools with me. I have no hammer. No saw. No chisel. And I am not sure tools would work. The embalmer is all skin. There is no hard place on him. He sees that I am looking at his skin. And he is smiling at me looking. He is smiling. At my face. He opens his arms. He says, And this is what I look like. He says, You are coming to see what I look like. The embalming room has a smell. Something dead that has not ever been alive. There are glass bottles on the shelf and the smell should be coming from them. There is fluid in all the bottles. But it is the embalmer that the smell is coming out of. He has the smell of something that has not ever been alive. The smell of something the sun should never touch. His face and its smile are closer. If there are no tools I do not know how to cut him. And Pearl's wrist is very ready. Though there is nothing to carve into. He is old. His face is all skin. But Pearl is made to cut him. He is her father and something in him makes her. Something in him makes his own death when it makes Pearl. And Pearl is really a cutter. She looks around the room and she sees tools. I see none. But Pearl is in me and she does. Her wrist takes one of the glass bottles from the embalmer's shelf. And her wrist smashes it. Like someone smashing a beer bottle against the main gate of Rose Head. And now there are shards of glass. And I have a long sharp piece. Rosmarge thinks she is teaching me the trade so that I can be a stonecutter. The new stonecutter for Marguerite Concrete. But she is also helping Pearl learn. Pearl is a good cutter and she becomes a better cutter. And now she is going to cut the embalmer. *Oh.* That is what the embalmer says. He is saying it very gently. He is looking at the shard of glass in my hand. Oh you know, you don't want to do that. And his smell is sweet and dead. He has not ever been alive. What is in the glass bottle is now on the floor. He sees me look at it. You know, he says, It's just the fluid. It can't hurt you. On the outside. When he says *On the outside* he smiles. He touches my elbow. It is my left elbow. Not the one next to Pearl's wrist. People in Little Neck like the embalmer. They don't understand why the sisters do not talk to their father. He is still touching my elbow. He likes to touch people. And he does it very gently. The skin of his fingers is on the skin of my elbow. He is a father and this must be the way a father touches. *You know how it is.* The air is cloudy in the embalming room. It is hard to think in this room. The embalmer's smell is clouding me. And the embalmer wants me to look at the part of his face that is making gentle words. At his lips and at his sharp little teeth. There is a shard of glass in my hand. And a sweeping feeling in Pearl's wrist. His fingers are moving a little on my elbow. You know, he says. He starts again, You know. He looks at my face and smiles. You have your mother's face. He stands closer. There is no sun in the room. Peggy's face exactly, he says. The embalmer keeps talking. He thinks that no cutting is going to happen if he is talking. But also he wants to talk. He wants to talk to me about his girls. You know, he says. I had five children. Four girls. The two older girls were good. They were good. The youngest oh she was a troublemaker. But your mother. Oh your mother was a very good girl. His fingers are on the skin of my wrist. And now on my elbow. His fingers are going up and down my arm. Touching my skin. The embalmer looks happy when he talks about the girls. The girls who are the sisters. And who are his children. The very good girl is the one who has my face. Peggy. He has a gentle voice. People in town like the embalmer and he is going to be dead soon. When he is dead Little Neck is the bereaved. And Little Neck picks his epitaph. Not the sisters. It is the town that is going to pick. Rosmarge is dead. Rita is busy with Rosmarge. Some in the town do not understand why the sisters do not talk to their father. Little Neck is going to pick the embalmer's epitaph and I know their pick. *In his care.* The embalmer talks in a gentle way. Calm. With care. And I am sure that he is very gentle when he embalms the bodies. If the bereaved watch him work they must say, How careful he is. He is good at touching. He is keeping his hand on my arm. He is the last person to touch the dead. The carpenter brings the box. The embalmer does his work. The lid closes. He is the last person to touch the dead. And some dead take a long time to die. They are not coughing or talking or breathing anymore. But it takes a very long time to die. Even after the last breath. The dead are still there and he is touching them in a gentle way. *In his care.* The embalmer keeps talking. Pearl's wrist is turned up toward the ceiling and the shard is ready. You know, the embalmer is saying. And he is smiling and gentle as he says it. You know you don't want to do that. And now Pearl also wants to talk to the embalmer. Pearl is saying something to him and she is saying it through my mouth. What she says is her name. *Pearl.* My mouth makes the letters. It is a small name and a small sound. It comes out of my mouth like a pebble. *Pearl.* Now the embalmer is looking at my mouth and not at Pearl's wrist. The shard is ready. *Pearl.* Oh, he says. He is close to me. He wants me to look at his voice and I do. Oh, he says. I see. Your aunt Pearl. What a troublemaker she was. He laughs a gentle laugh. He has a terrible smile. The bereaved like him. He says, You know the girls were very good. Rosmarge. Rita. Peggy. He has the gentlest laugh. But not Pearl, he says. Pearl was a troublemaker. He has no bottom lip and his teeth are small and sharp. He looks at my wrist but I don't think he knows it is Pearl's wrist. I cannot think with the embalmer near me. Touching me. His smell clouding me. But Pearl's wrist is ready. On the bindweed night at Pearl's grave a shard of glass cuts my wrist. That shard is thin at the top and rounded at the bottom. It is the shape of the shard that Pearl's wrist is holding now. But it is hard to think here. It is hard to know. The embalmer looks at the shard. He understands the question. He says, Oh I see. He takes his fingers away from the skin on my arm. He steps back and he shakes his head. Now he is very sad. He is sad because I am not understanding him. So he wants to tell the story of Pearl. Now he has his fingers on the skin of my arm again. He says, They say the youngest is the trouble-maker. And the older girls are not there anymore. Rosmarge takes Rita and they are off. They are taking over at Kucharski's. His cutting room. And then your mother goes. Peggy. Too soon. He stops talking. Then he starts again. And I just have Pearl at home with me now. Just Pearl. Around your age and she goes missing. The embalmer is so different from Rosmarge and Rita. All the embalmer does is talk. He talks like he has no secrets. There is nothing that is not good to say. He says every-thing. He keeps talking. Pearl's wrist is ready. The shard is ready. But the embalmer keeps talking. And you know she goes missing. Half of Little Neck is looking for her. He has a gentle laugh. He makes his laugh sad and gentle. You know she writes her name in the dirt. That's how we know it is her. Because it's hot. It's late summer when we find her you know. The body has decomposed a lot. But she writes her name in the dirt. She digs her own grave. Not deep mind you. And the embalmer laughs a gentle and sad laugh. Not a drop of rain that August. It says *Pearl* right there in the dirt when we find her. The body is so far gone. There's nothing I can do to preserve it. And that's that. He smiles with his mouth. It is hard to think in the embalming room. It is hard to think a thought through to its end. And Pearl's wrist is very ready. My first night at Marguerite Concrete the sisters say, He didn't get her. Do the sisters mean Pearl or do they mean me. The name Pearl is coming back up from my throat. It wants to be a pebble in my mouth. Pearl is going to say her name again. But I swallow it. I do not say it. There is still the puddle of fluid on the floor. The embalmer smiles. He has a sad smile and his breath smells dead. *He didn't get her.* Do the sisters mean Pearl or do they mean me. The embalmer is touching my arm. He is a father and this must be the way a father touches. *You know how it is.* But he does not get to touch Pearl. He wants to but she is not good. She is a trouble-maker. She runs away. And even when she is dead he does not get to touch her. He does not touch her hair and pull her head back. Or touch her lips to sew her mouth closed. He does not get to pull her shirt up to push the embalming fluid in. *He didn't get her.* The dirt is hard. She needs a shovel. And a pick. Groundskeepers' tools. The dirt is rocky at Rose Head. The rocks in the walls all around the cemetery come from the gravesites. The more dead the higher the walls grow. Pearl takes the digging tools from the groundskeeper's shed that night. And passes the chapelhouse window where the keeper is sitting. Where he folds his hands on his lap. His fingers touch the knuckles on the other hand. This is how he sleeps. This is how he is the last time I see him. I look through the chapel-house window. On the bindweed night. He is asleep. He is not listening. Pearl digs. Then cuts. Then lays herself in her grave.

And now the embalmer is going to let himself be cut. Now he is stepping back. He is taking steps back. Now he is at a slab. It is long and made of wood. He is smiling and lying down on the slab now. On his back like the dead. How's this, he says. I am standing over him. He is a help. He is trying to be a help. To lie down so that it is easier to cut him. It is worse that he is going to let me cut and he knows it is worse. He is on the slab and smiling up. He is a good father with a sad smile. And he has his fingers on my elbow again. This time it is the elbow that is connected to Pearl's wrist. His touch is gentle. But his gentleness is not good. He gets people with his gentleness. Most people in Little Neck like the embalmer. But the sisters do not. The embalmer gets Peggy. She was a very good girl. He gets Rosmarge and Rita. They were good girls. He gets them with his gentleness. He is a father and this must be his way. He tries to get Pearl but she was a troublemaker. And now he is on the slab where all the dead go before they go to Rose Head. Except for Rosmarge. Rita is not going to send Rosmarge here. And except for Pearl. She does not want her father touching her. She buries herself. She really is the smartest sister. Here now, the embalmer is saying. He is being helpful. He has a voice that is soft. It is a voice that asks to touch. With gentle fingers. Here now. He has his hand on my elbow. And he is moving his hand back and forth on my arm. From the shoulder to the elbow. Here now, he says. He is speaking more softly. I have to lean down to hear. His hand is gentle but it is also strong. He is a good father. It is a good feeling to have a hand move up and down my arm. Come here, he says. It is hard to think near him. Come here. He wants my face near his face. He is a good father and very gentle. It is hard to think. Pearl's wrist wants to do one thing. But I do not know if I want to do that thing. And then he says, Come here and be a good girl. And I let the pebble out of my mouth. *Pearl.* And he says it back. And it is not so gentle when he says it back. More air comes out of his mouth when he says her name this time. It is not good air. It is the bad smell of daisies. The dead sweet daisy smell. The embalmer is not gentle and he is not sad. But he is smiling. It is a bad smile. When I say Pearl he says Pearl back. But not gently. He does not like Pearl. He does not get her. He has a bad smile and I take his measure. I take his measure and Pearl starts the cut. She starts on one side of his smile. The cut loops under the chin and then across to the other side. A good first cut. But his smile is still on his face. *Thou beloved father.* That is what the embalmer says to me.

On the bindweed night at Pearl's grave there is a lot of blood coming out of my wrist. But it is dark and I am trying to get each runner and tuber and root. I don't see the blood. I faint. And then it is morning and the keeper finds me. His hands pull me out of her grave. He puts his hands under me. He carries me to the chapelhouse. This must be what happens. From Pearl's grave to the chapelhouse is five minutes of walking. The blood is coming out of me. Getting on his boots. But his hands are busy carrying me. He has to stop the blood with his mouth. His mouth is on my wrist. My wrist that is Pearl's wrist. He presses his mouth on the cut. To stop the blood. I can see his face. Some of the blood gets into his mouth. It is Pearl's wrist but it is my blood and my blood is happy to be in the keeper's mouth. And to be on his hands and on the skin of one side of his face. My blood is so happy it is crying into the keeper's knuckles and crying into the lines of his palm. It is trying to stay there. It wants to stay on his hands the way the dirt does. The keeper has his mouth on the cut. His hands are under me. He has to lean over as he walks. This must be what happens. He is leaning over with his mouth pressing on the cut. I have the tuber hand pressing inside and the keeper's mouth pressing outside. The keeper is hurrying. Trying to stop my blood with his mouth. His front teeth hit the bone of the wrist. And then he smells the peonies under my shirt. He remembers the Peggy stone. The day he says to me, Run. With his mouth on my cut the keeper starts to run. He runs and I wake up at Marguerite Concrete and he goes back to Rose Head and something happens. He leaves Little Neck. Or he dies. It is a long winter and then it is summer again and again winter. The slate dust is pollen. The gravestones are flowers. The cutting saw is the grass clippers. The carving tools are the air bugs. It is hard to carve into soft surfaces. And the embalmer is all skin. It is hard to carve the epitaph on his chest. He has so much skin and so much blood. But I have a good sweep going. I carve well with a shard. By the last letter the blood has stopped. The word goes from one side of his chest to the other. And the embalmer is dead. Pearl is over. And Rosmarge is over. Rosmarge is over. But I hear her. She is laughing and coughing at the epitaph on the embalmer's chest. *Father.* Rosmarge is laughing a lot at that word.

*H*E'S DEAD THEN IS HE, RITA SAYS. SHE IS AT THE door of the stonehouse watching me walk from up the road. The Chantilly is still on her from this morning. When I get to the doorway she looks at me. She looks small. Her cheeks do not crumble. The shard is in my hand. The hand connected to Pearl's wrist. But Pearl is over now. It is my wrist and my hand that hold the shard. And there is blood on my skin. So he's dead then, she says. Then she says, And the epitaph. It is the question she always asks. And the epitaph… Some of the bereaved can't talk and Rita is very good with them. When the bereaved cannot talk she says, Why don't you write it down. Why don't you write down what you want it to say. The shard is still in my hand and I carve the epitaph in the sand outside the door. *Father*. Rita reads the word out loud. Even though Rosmarge is always telling her not to say that word. She reads it out loud again. *Father*. Then she looks at my face. She is looking to see if I understand the epitaph. I am still outside the stone house. I see why the sisters do all the talking at the stone house door. The bereaved are more comfortable in a doorway. The bereaved want to leave. The bereaved want to say the same things over and over again until something different is at the end of what they say. And they are busy. They do not have a rest. They think that rest is coming. Rest is coming but it is far away. When the box is made and the dead buried and the ground set and the stone installed. And a year has passed. And the grass has grown in again around the stone. And the yellow gladioli are growing taller than the stone. Then the bereaved think they can rest. That their dead are dead. *Their names are preserved forever and their sleep is so peaceful.* That is what the bereaved think. Rita knows this is not true.

It is time to talk price. After the bereaved choose the stone size and the words then Rita talks price. Well then, she says. Talking price is something that Rita is not very good at. Rosmarge is better. Rita cannot hear as well as Rosmarge and the bereaved talk softly about price. But also Rosmarge is better at it. Sometimes Rita says, Well then. And Rosmarge hears her and steps up to the door. Now Rita says, Well then. And turns. She turns her head over her shoulder and Rosmarge is right there. Rosmarge is right there behind Rita. Her body is on the counter in the front room. And it is covered in concrete. There is no more of Rosmarge that is not concrete. Rita has been busy. She has mixed and poured and the concrete has started to set on Rosmarge. It is not a neat line. Her body is rocky. So Rita is not good with cement either. She is not a good cutter or carver or concrete finisher.

She does not make a brace to keep the form. She does not measure. The concrete she pours on her sister's body is not neat. Unlike the breasts that Rosmarge makes me. Which are smooth. They are small and neat and look like peonies. Rita looks at Rosmarge's body and says, It takes some time to set. I do not think that this is Rosmarge's plan. To have her body in concrete. The sisters are saving the cement to make gravestones. They plan that when Rita dies Rosmarge makes her a stone. It says her name but no family name. It says her dates. And then an epitaph. *Soon enough.* That's what Rosmarge picks for Rita. A message from Rosmarge to Rita. *Soon enough.* I can hear Rosmarge's voice saying it. Then Rosmarge dies first and Rita is not a carver. But Rita's plan is smarter. Rita's plan is much smarter. Now the embalmer can't get Rosmarge when she is dead. He gets her when she is alive and his daughter. But now she is dead and under concrete. He cannot get her with the embalming fluid. And the maggots can't get her and the air can't get her and the dirt can't eat her. There is so much dust in Rosmarge. If she is buried at Rose Head the dirt around her is going to turn to dust. And the dust to stone. In one hundred years Little Neck has a new quarry. It grows from Rosmarge's body. So it is better that she stays at Marguerite Concrete. To help Rita. Who is nodding at Rosmarge's body. She can still hear Rosmarge through the concrete. Rita is nodding. The sisters are talking price. They are talking the way they always talk. Rita says things and Rosmarge is under the concrete and does not say anything. And Rita understands what Rosmarge does not say. The sisters agree on a price. Rita turns back to me at the door and she says their price. It is not what I thought. I am not the one paying. It is Rita who is paying me. The embalmer is dead and I am the carver of his epitaph and she is paying me. She is paying me with one answer. I can ask the sisters any question and the question in me is *the keeper*. He finds me near a grave when I am left at Rose Head and he keeps me. He finds me at a grave again but I am bleeding and he gives me to the sisters. And then. What happens. Where does the keeper go. But *the keeper* is not the question that comes out of my mouth. What comes out of me is different. *Peggy*. I have never heard the sisters say her name. But I am saying it. That is my question and that is my price. Rita's hearing is not good. I have to say it again. *Peggy*. Now Rita looks very small. It is a very high price that I am asking. It is so high that Rosmarge is refusing to pay it. Her body is rocky and large. Rosmarge's body is there under the famous Marguerite Concrete but now Rita is alone in the room. She is small and my price is high. She turns and goes to the side-board. It is where the sisters keep their papers. She comes back with something in her hands. It is a ball of something small and gray. I drop the shard and touch the thing in Rita's hands. It is a pair of mittens. Very small. Too small for Rita. Too small for me. But they are mine. They are mine from when I am born. Rita says, She left you with us. But Rosmarge said this wasn't a good place for a baby. The dust. Better to be in the chapelhouse. And outside. And he agreed. But we forgot to pack these. We get back and these are on the sideboard. And I say, Rosmarge. And she sees these. But we had already said goodbye. This wasn't a good place for a baby. Rosmarge said it was better to be in the chapelhouse. And outside. And he agreed. Peter agreed. She left you with us. She didn't ask Peter. But Rosmarge said this wasn't a good place for a baby. The dust. The tools are loud. And he agrees. She doesn't ask Peter. She leaves you with us. But then we leave you with him. It's better. We are going to leave you with him. And we say goodbye and we get back and these are on the sideboard. I see them. I say, Rosmarge. She sees them too. Rita takes the mittens out of my hand. There is more in her to say. But now it is not her voice coming out of her. It is the embalmer's voice. The embalmer is over but his voice is not. His voice is so gentle it gets inside me. I cannot stop hearing him. It gets inside Pearl. She has to cut her wrist open to get it out. And his voice is still inside Rita. Now she is talking the way he does. In a gentle voice. It is very gentle and terrible. She says, Rosmarge and I. We were good girls. She closes her eyes. Rosmarge's body is still. Rosmarge is not going to give any answers. Or this is her answer. It is not a good answer. It is a high price and Rita and Rosmarge do not seem to be paying it. Rita says, Pearl was the trouble-maker. Rosmarge and I were good. And Peggy. Peggy was very good. Peggy was a very good girl. Rita still has her eyes closed. Not gently closed. Closed hard. But they are trying to open. And then they do. Her eyes open and the stones start coming out. Not pebbles. Large stones. Rita is a hill and large stones are rolling off her. I am trying to leave. It is time to go back to Rose Head. *Until the day breaks and the shadows flee.* To close the door and leave. The large stones from her eyes are blocking the door. Rita is taking my hand. She is pulling me back inside the stone house. We go past Rosmarge's body and into Rita's bedroom. I am going to help her. She wants her bed in the front room. Her bed next to Rosmarge's body. The embalmer is dead and the doors do not need to be locked. Rita can die now. She is going to mix her cement. Her bag has hundreds of pounds. A little less. She uses some to stop the bleeding on my wrist my first night. And when I pull up the peonies Rosmarge uses a handful to make the new breasts. But hundreds of pounds are left. Rita says over and over as she mixes, The hour is late I cometh. She is talking to Rosmarge. *The hour is late I cometh*. It is an epitaph on one of the old graves. The slate is cracked. The rain has washed the deep carve away. It is an epitaph you have to read with your fingers. *The hour is late I cometh*. The dying are not going. They are coming. It takes Rita a very long time to mix the cement. It takes all night. The town is going to find the embalmer. And then they are going to find Rosmarge. And Rita. The rain comes. The quarryman's daughter feels it in her dead elbow and then it comes. And Rita lies down on her bed. She still has the Chantilly on. I am wearing thick gloves. Concrete burns, Rita says. I start the pour on Rita's legs. It's good to go fast but the buckets are heavy. Now it's her chest. Rita says to Rosmarge, She hath done what she could. And she laughs. And Rosmarge laughs. The concrete on Rosmarge's chest moves like she is laughing. The concrete on Rita's chest starts to set. It is heavy. I wait for her to say something. Her little eyes are closed. Then her mouth opens. But I am already starting the pour on her neck. Her mouth opens. Maybe it is opening to laugh. Or it is opening because of the pain. Or it is opening to speak. But the bucket is too heavy to stop quickly. The concrete goes into her open mouth and down her throat. The famous Marguerite Concrete. *Now go.*

ROSE HEAD IS ONLY HALF A MILE. I DON'T GO IN
through the main gate. I go through the woods. I enter
Rose Head at the top of the hill where the old oaks are.
Where some kids in Little Neck come to drink at night.
They don't cross over the rock wall into the cemetery. But
we hear them at night. I go through those woods and climb
over the wall. It is summer. An afternoon. Summer coming. It is summer and summer is coming. The old oaks by
the rock wall look small. The white pines look small. And
the grass is not the color I remember. The peonies start
to hurt when I am standing on the hill. Where my skin
and the concrete are mixed. The ground of my chest. And
also the tips of the peony breasts hurt. Though they are
concrete. It is the summer of the trouble again. And they
are growing. And hurting. Though now they are made of
concrete. I feel the buds opening. Like the day at Peggy's
grave. When the keeper touches me. The day I am hiding. To be found. I hide by the gravestone with the white

peonies. The stone that says *Peggy*. And beneath, *In sorrow across eternity*. I hide there inside the white peony bush. I put my shirt behind the gravestone. And in the bush I make an arch. My knees beside *Sorrow* and my hands and feet in the dirt. My shoulder is next to *Eternity*. My eyes are next to the letters NI. *NI*. I know now it is Rosmarge who carves them. I am an arch. An arch inside the peony bush. And the two peonies where my breasts would be are at the top of the bush. Now I do not have knees. I do not have shoulders. I am breathing the way the flower breathes. I keep reading the two letters. *NI*. I breathe and stay still. And the keeper comes. He visits all the peony bushes on June afternoons. And the white are his favorite. He walks toward the gravestone. His boots drag. I am an arch. I am reading *NI* and hear the keeper bending down. The keeper loves peonies. The white ones. I am breathing. *NI*. His hand makes a circle. His whole hand around the bud. He puts his hands around and under the flowers. His eyelids are holding up dirt. Now the dirt is too heavy. His eyes close. The skin on his palms is warm. And his mouth is warm. Warmer than his hands. He smells things with his mouth. One peony on me is a bud and then it is not. Then it is breaking open. There is a sound. Like sifting soft dirt. His eyelids. The dirt is off them. The lids are up. He sees the peony breaking open. It is the warmness of his hand doing it. And then he sees me. In an arch. A bad arch. Something to laugh at. He sees that I have two flowers where the breasts would be. And that one flower is in his hand. That the petals are wet from his mouth. Then he says something. His voice is full of dirt. I do not understand. His hand is still around the flower. His mouth is very close. He says it again. *Run.* I remember one day when I am little and the keeper is kneeling on the east cape hill. On the dead grass and old snow. He is scraping algae from a stone. I am sliding down the hill. Coming back up. Rolling down the hill again. My body stops rolling. I put my mouth on some old snow and bite it. Ice on the tongue. But then. There is a white mouth inside my mouth. A white mouth is coming out of the ground. It is cold and dry. My mouth has a dead mouth inside it. The keeper comes down the hill. He takes the maggot mouth out of my mouth. He has his gloves on. I am seeing the cloth on his fingers. The lips of the thing are together. Just the lips of the mouth are coming out of the dirt. But there has to be a whole dead body below it. The lips are the lips of a dead face on a dead body. Now the keeper puts his hand around it. *Crocus.* He says the word out loud. I hear his voice. *Cro-cus. NI.* He sees that the peony in his hand is mine. *Run.* I run down to the paupers' part. Into the high grass. I run so fast I breathe in two grass flies and they stick in my throat. The sun is still strong. The grass is high. I have no shirt on. I am trying to cough the grass flies back out. I cough until fluid comes up from my stomach. A bright green fluid. A peony green. But the two grass flies do not come up. They are married in me. I am kneeling in the grass and covering the fluid with more grass. My elbows bang my chest and hurt the peonies. So I bang them more. It is so good to hurt them. A stick from the crabapple tree. I push the stick into the middle of one flower and then the other. Then go and knock on the chapelhouse door and the keeper opens it and sees. Blood and flower juice running down my chest. Now I am back at Rose Head and the peonies are hurting. I go to the chapelhouse and knock on the door.

The sun is strong. The air is wet and smells of salt. And when the door opens I can smell the coolness inside the chapelhouse. It is an old man who comes. Old as the embalmer. He opens the door. The chapelhouse is where the cemetery groundskeeper lives. There is no chapel here anymore. It is just rooms for the groundskeeper. An old man answers the door. His knuckles have dirt very deep in them. His fingernails are short and have green beneath them. He is the groundskeeper. It is easy to tell when I see his hands. But he is not my keeper. What do you want. I am standing in the doorway. He says, What do you want kid. The last time I am standing outside this door it is the keeper on the other side. I am opening the door and going in. The keeper's hand is on the inside knob. He is just pushing the door open to come out. Oh, he says. His eyelids go up and back down quickly. He has looked at me. I have looked at him too. That is the summer of the trouble. It is after the peonies. When I am near the keeper he goes as still as the dead. At dinner in the chapelhouse we are eating at the same table and he does not look up. He is dead over his plate. He is dead and I am the bereaved. Every dinner. In sorrow across eternity. I say it over my plate. *In sorrow across eternity.* When my mouth says *Sorrow* it opens a little bit longer than when it says other words. Sorrow. He is alive and looking across at me. I look up. No his eyes are down. He is dead over his plate. I say it again. *Sorrow.* I keep my mouth open long enough for his mouth to come into mine. Then *eternity*. And the keeper's tongue clicks the *T* and *N* and *T* on the smooth top of my mouth. What do you want kid. It is the new keeper. His voice has no dirt in it. It is a tired voice. He is an old man. He looks up at the sky. It is late afternoon. He says, The cemetery closes at five. He says, Which is soon. So scram. The door closes. Now go.

The Viti graves are on the hill in the main part of Rose Head. Pearl's grave is very far from the Viti ones. Hers is on the east cape closer to the sea. In the older part of the cemetery. And Peggy's grave is in the main part but down the hill. Closer to the paupers' part. I know Pearl buries herself. But I do not know why Peggy is not with the other Vitis. Someone in Little Neck has to pick a different place for Peggy. Maybe it is the embalmer. Peggy is so good she gets a special place. Or it is Rita and Rosmarge. Peggy is their sister and *Viti* is a word that makes dust in their mouths. Or it is the keeper. Peggy gets a plot where peonies grow well. When I live at Rose Head I do not go near the Viti graves. Daisies do not need keeping. And they smell like death. And I do not know the Vitis are my people. The keeper never says. It is warm. I am in the sun on the grass. This is on a day a long time ago. A day when I do not know about the sisters. Or the Vitis. I am new. This is before the summer of the trouble. I go up to the east cape and sit on the hill. I am inside the sun and inside the green and the green is loud. I almost hear what it is saying. The keeper is pushing the mower. It is the first time cutting the grass that year. I have the feeling that I should know something. I do not know what. I take a piece of grass from the hill and one crabapple blossom and one piece of my hair. I put them in a pocket of the old rock wall in the main part. But then it snows. A late snow. It surprises the keeper. The tulips do not die but the early tree blossoms do. The rock walls are covered for two days. Then the snow melts. My things are gone. They slide away with the melting snow. I pick new things. Grass again. A pine needle. And the loose skin from around my thumb's nail. This time I put them in my mouth. That is the way to know and to keep. With the fingers and the mouth. I did not want to know I was a Viti. I wanted to think I could be a flower. At the Viti graves there is bindweed. That is the first thing I see. Bindweed and it is deep. It winds around the daisies. Its vines are touching the graves. There is one grave that is thin and tall and the bindweed winds around the whole stone. The graves do not say much. *Viti*. And the first names. And the dates. One in the front has an epitaph. *Death is always nigh*. Bindweed is so pretty. The white and pink flowers. Each side of the leaves curling in toward the other. It is very pretty. But it strangles. This bindweed at the Viti plot has been here a long while. There is much more bindweed here than at Pearl's grave two years ago. The new keeper has not seen it. Or he has seen it and he is tired. Soon the embalmer is going to be buried here. And his bad fluids are going to leak out of his box. His mouth smells like daisies and daisies smell like death. The fluids from his glass bottles are in the embalmer. And they leak out of his box. The grass near the Viti graves comes up yellow. A sick yellow. And the bindweed flowers dry up. The roots die and the tubers stop digging down. Little Neck moves Rosmarge's body to the cemetery. And Rita's. The town gets a hoist and a crane and moves the sisters. To the Viti plot. There is no one to say otherwise. And the new keeper plants baneberry on top of Rita. Its berries look like the eyes of the newly dead. Its berries see everything. And on top of Rosmarge the new keeper plants a holly bush. The leaves prickle. And the holly grows even in dust. The concrete around the sisters crumbles when it is buried. Some summers pass. And the dirt around the Vitis turns to sand... And here is the keeper. I am looking at him for a long time before I see him. His stone. It says *Groundskeeper* at the bottom. And above that it says his dates. And above those, *P. Viti.* I look at the dates for a long time before I see them. First I see *Groundskeeper.* Then *P. Viti.* The keeper's grave. And he has a name. A first name that starts with P. And a last name. So the keeper is a Viti. So he is also a Viti. I see the dates and now I have to read them. I am reading the first date and I think the keeper is born around the time of Rosmarge and Rita. Peter. The brother. On my first night at Marguerite Concrete the sisters think I am asleep. And Rosmarge says, She is a quiet one. And Rita says, Just like Peter. My first night the sisters want to talk about the keeper. They ask a lot about him. And then they never say a thing about him again. Which means there is something to say. And now I have to read the date of death. It is a day two years ago. In August. My last day at Rose Head. The day I wake up at Marguerite Concrete is the day the keeper dies. Rosmarge locks the doors all the time. The front and back doors. The basement bulkhead. She does not want me to be gotten. She does not want the embalmer to try and find me. Or she does not want me to try and find the keeper. To find that the keeper is dead. Rosmarge is the town's only carver. And no other carver from another town helps. I know Rosmarge's work. I can see her making the *i*'s in Viti. I am lying on the long couch in the sideroom. My wrist is bleeding. It is my second day at Marguerite Concrete and Rosmarge is in the back room beginning to carve a gravestone for the keeper. Who is a Viti. The sisters do not say a thing. It is better to never say or ask a thing at all. And Rosmarge is dead. And Rita. And the embalmer. And Pearl's wrist. There is no one to ask about the keeper. How he dies. Or there is everyone to ask. Half of Little Neck. Half the town maybe knows. But what the town knows it does not like to say. And the town listens to what sounds good. Like the embalmer's voice. Which is gentle and kind. It is the embalmer who says that Pearl digs her own grave. And the embalmer who says she cuts her own wrist. He says she is a troublemaker. And Rosmarge and Rita say it too. But there is a lot they do not know. I hold the shard in my hand that night. I see the bottle at the embalmer's and remember the shape of that shard. I don't like talking. Or listening. But then I hear someone talking to me. It is Rosmarge. Her voice. It is in my ear. She is dead at Marguerite Concrete but her voice is here at Rose Head with me. In my ear. She is saying, Time to cut. The cemetery is getting dark. I remember how to hold the shed door to stop its squeak. And where the pruning saw is. And the shovel and the pick. I bring them back to the Viti plot. I am digging all night. Through the bindweed roots. Which break. And are going to multiply. And now it is almost morning. Almost morning but still dark. Even in the dark I can see well. And I can see right away that the embalmer has not touched the keeper's body. It is the jaw that shows me. The embalmer wires jaw bones together. The skin on the keeper's neck is gone. His mouth is gone. But his jaw is open. No wires. No embalmer. No embalmer means something. Someone has to say, No embalmer. And people in Little Neck like the embalmer. They think he is gentle and easy to listen to. It has to be Rosmarge and Rita who say, No embalmer. When the keeper dies it has to be the sisters who keep him from the embalmer. Which means they must be his bereaved. I am lying on the couch in the side room at Marguerite Concrete when he dies. He finds me at Pearl's grave and brings me to the sisters and dies. Bereaved of me. Or he finds me in the grave. Nightclothes full of blood. He has to take care of things. He has to touch me. He brings me to the sisters and dies. From having touched me. Touching me is what he wanted. Or not what he wanted. He wants to touch me because he is a Viti and they do that. Or he does not want to touch me because he does not want to be like a Viti. He carries me to Marguerite Concrete and smells the peonies on my chest and remember that day at the Peggy stone and dies. From touching a flower growing from me and not a flower growing from Peggy. He finds me at Pearl's grave with blood on my peonies. He takes me to Marguerite Concrete and dies. In sorrow across eternity. He finds me in the dirt with Pearl's bones. And he knows Pearl. She is a Viti and he is a Viti. And he brings me to Marguerite Concrete where Rosmarge says to him, Now go. And Rosmarge is his sister and listens to her and goes and dies. He finds me at Pearl's grave and brings me to the sisters. They are his sisters and they have questions for him. But he never wants to say a thing at all. He dies. On the bindweed night he finds me at Pearl's grave. There are five tuber fingers inside me. Five fingers that smell like dirt and look like skin. A tuber hand. He pulls it out. It looks like his hand. He dies. He is dead but he brings me to Marguerite Concrete and when I wake up I hear the sisters say it. *He didn't get her.* It is almost morning at Rose Head. The keeper's box is open and I have the pruning saw. Rosmarge's voice in my ear, Time to cut. It is easy to saw off the keeper's wrist bone. I cut off his hand at the wrist. And I am careful with the bones of his fingers. They are still together and I want them to stay that way. For a little longer. And now his box is closed. The dirt is back on top. And a pile of bindweed on top of the dirt. But the smell is no good here. It is the shasta daisies. And it is cold here. The Viti plot is half shade and half sun but it is as cold as inside the stonehouse. When I walk down through the high grasses of the paupers' part all the air bugs fly up into the sun. The air is warmer here. And the birds are loud. And the green is loud. The morning grass is wet but not cold. I do not know if I am here in the grass to sleep or to wake up. *Rose upon the horizon of a perfect endless day.* I have the keeper's hand bones in my hand

and I am awakening at Rose Head. *He giveth his beloved sleep.* Or I have the keeper's thumb bone in my mouth and I am going to close my eyes. I am here in the high grass but I do not know if it is to wake up or to sleep. The keeper's fingers are making a circle. His whole hand around the bud. Now it is concrete and not petals. Now it is bones and not skin. But the keeper loves my peonies. He puts his hand around the flower.

FONO GRAᖆ

1. **Eileen Myles**—*Aloha/irish trees* (LP)

2. **Rae Armantrout**—*Conflation* (LP)

3. **Alice Notley**—*Live in Seattle* (LP)

4. **Harmony Holiday**—*The Black Saint and the Sinnerman* (LP)

5. **Susan Howe & Nathaniel Mackey**—*STRAY: A Graphic Tone* (LP)

6. **Annelyse Gelman & Jason Grier**—*About Repulsion* (EP)

7. **Joshua Beckman**—*Some Mechanical Poems To Be Read Aloud* (print)

8. **Dao Strom**—*Instrument/ Traveler's Ode* (print; cassette tape)

9. **Douglas Kearney & Val Jeanty**—*Fodder* (LP)

10. **Mark Leidner**—*Returning the Sword to the Stone* (print)

11. **Charles Valle**—*Proof of Stake: An Elegy* (print)

12. **Emily Kendal Frey**—*LOVABILITY* (print)

13. **Brian Laidlaw and the Family Trade**—*THIS ASTER: adaptations of Emile Nelligan* (LP)

14. **Nathaniel Mackey and The Creaking Breeze Ensemble**—*Fugitive Equation* (compact disc)

15. *FE Magazine* (print)

16. **Brandi Katherine Herrera**—*MOTHER IS A BODY* (print)

17. **Jan Verberkmoes**—*Firewatch* (print)

18. **Krystal Languell**—*Systems Thinking with Flowers* (print)

19. **Matvei Yankelevich**—*Dead Winter* (print)

20. **Cody-Rose Clevidence**—*Dearth & God's Green Mirth* (print)

Fonograf Editions is a registered 501(c)(3) nonprofit organization. Find more information about the press at: fonografeditions.com.